A Whale Watcher's Guide

to the Apocalypse

A Novel

BY

Lewis Evans

Deux Voiliers Publishing

Ian Thomas Shaw, editor

Ian Thomas Shaw, interior and cover designer

Christina Nick, cover art

Deux Voiliers Publishing

Gatineau, Québec

www.deuxvoilierspublishing.com

First edition

Printed in Canada

Legal Deposit

Library and Archives Canada Cataloguing in Publication
Title: A Whale Watcher's Guide to the Apocalypse : a
Novel / by Lewis Evans.
Names: Evans, Lewis (Author of A whale watcher's guide
to the apocalypse), author.
Identifiers: Canadiana 20230196470 | ISBN
9781928049586 (softcover)
Classification: LCC PS8609.V3865 W53 2023 | DDC
C813/.6—dc23

TO PIM

Casualty of accidental heroics, bulwark against teetotalism
and other manifestations of tyranny, grudging protagonist
of *City Upon a Hill* and *El Salvador Breathless*.

Public opinion remained divided. At least until the big stuff went down. After that people had other worries. Serious ones. Like where to find water, living without a credit card, how to most profitably pimp yourself or your sister, keeping a low profile under occupation by a foreign power, etc. But before all that and for the better part of a long and glorious summer, the Frontiersman's activities separated Canadians into two opposing camps. With each daring exploit or cheap antic, the trench between rural and urban Canada deepened.

"Yerrrr! Fucking right!" people living in the country were prone to say. "Who can blame 'em for not wanting to be a desticle? A life spent pushing paper like some shuffle-butt cube jockey. Might as well as shoot yerself."

Proponents of this line of reasoning would then eye the row of beer bottles they'd polished off earlier that morning, take a few steadying breaths and get on with target practice. Only the fewest of these country dwellers were actual farmers. Most got by on welfare, from growing marijuana or part-time jobs at the local Canadian Tire store. The mere fact, however, that they owned lawnmowers, spent their lives in rubber boots and didn't hate snow shovelling enough to seek refuge in a condo made them fundamentally different from their city-dwelling peers. Other realities of country living, country, not country club, deepened this city-vs-boondocks divide and strengthened the rural sense of identity. The thrill, for instance, of speeding down a country road while blind drunk at the age of twelve in your cousin's pickup. The cousin who leaves the keys in the ashtray can't object because they're doing time for stealing someone's riding lawnmower. Or hot tub. Or the right of passage of shooting not only at a beer can but at something living, a deer or a dog, and watching it buckle and slump lifelessly to the ground. Or, if you were a lousy shot or had enjoyed a breakfast of Great Lakes Lager, watch it slink away to die a lonely and painful death. Hard to be confronted with life's essential cruelty in an on-the-leash dog park.

Cultural differences mattered too. How many people who ride the bus to their government jobs each morning can claim to have had their teeth kicked in in bars that only serve generic bottled beer? Beer brewed not in quaint microbreweries with shiny copper vats but in giant factories owned by faceless conglomerates? Or had sex with a waitress who was a childhood friend of their mom's because the waitress was the only person in the bar they hadn't already slept with and said it made her feel young again? The answer is very few. In short, something about the imperfection and the joys of country living made country folk more comfortable with trial and error and with the Frontiersman's dogged, if not always linear, pursuit of freedom. Or meaning. Or something.

Naturally, this doesn't mean that city dwellers didn't spend their every waking hour plotting how to have sex with strangers they'd just met online. As a matter of fact, besides pushing paper in cubicles, drinking expensive coffees, or swiping at their phones while eating ethnic take-out food on couches that matched the above-couch lithograph, this was the only thing they did do. That is until the age of about thirty for women and thirty-five to sixty-five for men. Only then did the average urbanite stop thinking only about themselves and begin copulating with a purpose. The purpose of starting a family. One which would have at most one, soon-to-be spoiled rotten child.

The rampant promiscuity that had transformed Canadian metropolises into hotbeds of sexually transmitted diseases was, therefore, not what made city dwellers take a more negative view of the Frontiersman's lawless behaviour than their rural peers. Later studies conducted by reputable centers of higher learning concluded that the desire to lay blame and point fingers had other roots.

Listening to the CBC, for instance. Empirical data showed that anyone exposed to more than ten seconds a day of CBC believed that the world was a fair place based not on hard knocks and conflicting visions fighting it out to the death but on feelings. Hordes of bylaw enforcing officers and a generalized culture of concerned citizens policing themselves and others also contributed to an environment that was as asepticized as it was unforgiving. Imagine never being able to break or at least bend the law. For instance, by letting your dog off the leash, pretending to not see it shit all over and breezily strolling away instead of stooping and scooping. Not ideal, especially not for the person who steps in the shit or the mother who pushes her stroller through it and then stores the stroller in the trunk of her Subaru Outback, but also not the end of the world. Shit happens, after all.

In short, extreme societal constraints made people tense and eager to pass judgment on others, particularly in a city like Ottawa.

Part I

Awakening

If it takes 10 to 20 pounds of force to crush an empty beer can, and the bite of a blue whale is 19 000 PSI, and the home range of the solitary wolverine can vary between 100 and 600 square miles, what is X, and why, not Y, and why not? – unresolved theorem.

A-Woke

The Frontiersman is the name the press eventually gave him. His real name, his background, cute childhood photos, a trauma that might have nudged him over the edge: no amount of guesswork, cyber sleuthing or actual police work was able to wrest these details from the realm of speculation. What were his dreams, motivations, political orientation and diverse skill set that included bingo, communing with the natural world and welding? And what about his ability to consume impressive amounts of alcohol and still function or appear to function? Not to mention his physical location, which, much to the chagrin of law enforcement, remained a mystery.

Clear was only that the Frontiersman didn't live in a high-rise condo. He lived in the basement apartment of a building that was never meant to have a basement apartment. The only difference between the Frontiersman's apartment and a regular, low-ceilinged, dingy basement was that someone, his landlord or the slumlord his landlord had bought the building from, had somehow gotten a stove, toilet and front door down the narrow stairs.

The last time the Frontiersman awoke in the bedroom of his basement apartment—his last yawn and Dutch oven flatulence marking some kind of day zero—his sleepy gaze rested on the cheap sliding doors of his closet. Like everything else in the apartment, the closet doors are the crummiest version of closet doors money can buy. The left one had once again derailed.

Instead of getting out of bed, the Frontiersman prefers to stay under the covers and imagine what lies ahead. He sees himself sifting through the heap of rumpled office clothes. The shirt he'd choose wouldn't have to be spotless; it just couldn't reek, and the pants needed to be free of chicken wing sauce. His manager had commented. Next, he'd move into the kitchen, ducking to pass below the heating ducts that pumped warm or cold air to the upper units that enjoyed regular ceiling heights. With unfounded hope in his heart, he'd open the refrigerator. Then he'd close the fridge and open the kitchen cupboard where the granola bars were kept. Or the empty boxes that once contained granola bars.

Knowing that the feeling of being in control of one's life began with small acts, he'd turn his back on the defeats of the kitchen and move to the bathroom. Here he'd brush his teeth with an extra soft toothbrush intended to keep gums from receding. Or from receding further. Unlike the fresh-faced, go-get-'em characters that starred in men's skincare ads and loved their reflections, the Frontiersman would quietly avert his eyes while applying hair gel to his ambitious widow's peak. Morning grooming would be followed with a morning bout of wrestling with the front fucking door lock the landlord refused to fix. Then he'd hold his breath while ascending the stinky rear staircase and two blocks later be at the bus stop that, like every other day, was crammed with other people, other people just like him.

The still-horizontal Frontiersman closes his eyes tighter. The Frontiersman who spends the next forty minutes swaying and being jostled in a crammed bus notices he's not the only one to wear his shirts more than once. Eventually, the bus crosses to the Quebec side of the Ottawa River and disgorges its human freight among the fortress-like government buildings that occupy the waterfront.

Because the Frontiersman thinks six dollars for a cup of coffee is abhorrent, he doesn't bother imagining standing in line at the local fair-trade coffee shop that does brisk business with his profligate colleagues. Instead, he envisions buying a very large and very cheap cup of drip coffee from the Vietnamese lady who runs the uninspiring cafeteria in the lobby of his building. The Frontiersman, who's still in bed, relishes the thought of his daily purchase of half a gallon of warm and milky coffee in a styrofoam cup the size of a bucket.

"For less than a dollar," he mutters contently, his voice groggy with sleep but not unpleasant. He gives his pillow a loving squeeze.

If the other Frontiersman thinks of the building in which he works, an unadorned monolith and aesthetic abomination, as *his* building, then only because he's been dragging himself through its front doors and into its bowels for longer than he cares to remember. *His* building is flanked on all sides by other government high-rises, democratic in their mediocrity and drabness. Although his forays into the adjacent eyesores have been limited, he

3

assumes they house other branches of government. This makes the Frontiersman wonder when the word 'branch' was hijacked by governments to describe not the living, growing, and leaf-sprouting limb of a sapling but a beetle-infested scrawny offshoot of some long dead trunk.

Although the Frontiersman isn't asleep, he wishes he were, hits snooze and pretends. It does him no good. The truth will out. A giant centipede of city buses disgorging anonymous, government ID sporting hordes into the wasteland through which he has blundered for decades writhes before his inner eye.

"No!" he shouts, burrowing deeper into his yellow-tinged, waxy bedding.

The enemy's advance is relentless. There are policy makers, policy coordinators, policy planners, policy specialists and policy revisers, who are the people who undo previously accomplished work. But also throngs of others, many with serious seniority and paygrades, who should have been fired decades ago. Despite their sheer numbers that darken the horizon or at least both sidewalks of Taché Boulevard from the Tim Hortons on Eddy Street to the corner of Laval, the Frontiersman knows this festering colony of worker ants is but a tiny cog in the machinery of government. Feeling faint, the Frontiersman pokes his nose out from under the covers and wonders if such a puny wheel can turn anything. Or whether it goes round and round on its own with no effect on anything else. He pictures the mechanism behind the face of a Swiss watch in which precision and purpose are united. When he compares Swiss watchmaking to his government work, he cannot find a single parallel.

Disgusted, he lets his eyes rove across the bedside table. A once fashionable now has-been IKEA lamp, a half-read Wilbur Smith paperback on top of the V.S. Naipaul novel he's been meaning to read, a box of Kleenex, a uniform layer of dust. An amber-coloured blur on the underside of the bedside table forces his pupils to contract. A booger swims into focus. Revolting, but the Frontiersman knows only he can have put it there. If the last woman who shared his bed stuck the bogey there, it would belong in a museum. Why isn't there anyone sharing his bed?

Instead of removing the dried nasal mucus or confronting uncomfortable questions about his love life and life, he averts his gaze. A mistake. It lands harshly on his government ID card. The Frontiersman stares at his laminated face, which stares back. It's a regular face. Sufficiently symmetrical, crowned by enough hair, especially if swept forward, jawline instead of jowls. It's the eyes where things fall apart. The eyes that looked into whatever camera took the picture and now stare accusingly at the Frontiersman are two black holes. Deep wells that reach far beyond the water table, tunnelling to hell and maybe beyond. If the embalmers of Egyptian pharaohs weren't in the habit of removing the eyes of their recently deceased despots, their eyes would be his eyes. Not self-assured and imperious eyes as might be expected of kings with the status of Gods who enjoyed falconry, slave harems and sheets of Egyptian cotton, but eyes that spent the last three thousand years staring at the inside of a coffin. He shudders involuntarily and tries to clear his mind.

5

Another mistake. Yves Gagnon, a colleague whose specialty is calculating the number of days separating fellow colleagues from retirement, appears unbidden before the Frontiersman's mind's eye.

"Seven thousand eight hundred and sixty-four," Yves had concluded.

After palming Yves off on an intern, a hasty calculation translated the number into twenty-one and a half more years of work. Or more years of showing up and going through the motions of work. More years of Yves too. Despite Yves' number being lower, much lower. Retirement and death jockeyed for pole position in Yves' immediate future. After a career spent wasting the time of his colleagues and the nation's tax dollars, Yves was excited about the upcoming changes. Not to mention strangely indifferent to the order in which they might occur.

"*Au moins ça change,*" Yves would tell anyone he cornered at the coffee machine, urinal or photocopier.

The thought of Yves is the last straw. The mummy's eyes snap open, any trace of dullness has vanished from their gaze. The Frontiersman throws back his sheets and moments later exits his basement apartment. His government ID remains in the basement. Having slipped from the bedside table in the tumult of the Frontiersman throwing on clothes, it now rests on a pile of used Kleenex on the floor, that attest to the Frontiersman's loneliness and vivid imagination.

Outfitting

The Frontiersman wheels his bicycle out of the garage and rides West down Donald Street, slaloming potholes, until he reaches the Vanier Parkway. He pushes the crosswalk button and waits. The Vanier Parkway is the demarcation line between the right and wrong side of the Rideau River. Vanier, the neighbourhood the Frontiersman calls home, a blighted urban fabric without parks or a main street, historically poor, Francophone, and now rife with drugs and the violence that can't stay away from drugs, is the wrong side. The Frontiersman watches as hundreds of cars speed past. He wonders where everyone is going. Are they all driving back to the suburbs after a Vanier drug run? Eventually, the light turns green, and the Frontiersman cycles on. He crosses the Rideau River and bikes through Sandy Hill's student ghetto, where once stately homes have been subdivided into insalubrious but profitable warrens of prison-cell-sized rooms and communal kitchens of unspeakable hygiene.

Reaching the Rideau Canal, a man-made waterway of which both banks are highly desirable, the Frontiersman merges into the bike path's heavy traffic. He is overtaken by deadpan joggers strapped to heart-rate monitors and lean department of justice lawyers riding titanium racing bikes. Traffic lightens once the bike path passes the downtown strongholds of government employment, and aspiring deputy vice managers yield to leisure-seekers and, because it's ten in the morning, to the unemployed and homeless. The Frontiersman follows the bike path to the Ottawa River. He turns West, upstream and passes below the Supreme Court and the National Archives that sit on a bluff. A tangle of small islands that once housed a paper mill now feature a lookout point, brew pub and hydroelectric dam. He changes gears and accelerates through faint signs of gentrification that nibble at Chinatown. His steady cadence carries him past the hovels of Mechanicsville that the Ottawa real estate boom has dolled up with en-vogue metal siding and gallons of paint in sombre but regal tones. The expression *to put lipstick on a century-old termite-infested pig* comes to mind. The Frontiersman's mind.

"You'd gotta be nuts to pay half a million for one of these dumps," he thinks, looking around.

Suddenly his front tire skids through a smear of Canada goose turd. Luck, dexterity and foul language keep him upright.

"Serves me right," he chastises himself, refocusing on the dangers of the road ahead.

What does he care if satin finish paint jobs and cedar fencing are enough to convince people to pay fortunes for basement-less shacks? He swerves expertly around other dark green turds and wonders what geese eat for their turds to be this colour. Is he eating enough greens? Ten minutes later, he locks his bike to the rack in front of Ottawa's Premier outdoor outfitter.

What has brought the Frontiersman to this mecca of gear is unclear. His plans are far from certain. Fact is, he has no plan. He is going purely on gut instinct, and his gut tells him he's gonna need stuff and a lot of it. He yanks a shopping cart that is part of a conga line of shopping carts, but the carts are stuck together and don't budge. He yanks again with greater force, but the cart refuses to be separated from its brethren. He enters the store with not one but five trolleys.

A store employee wishes him a great day. Hesitant to jinx things, the Frontiersman does not respond. Not one to dither when his mind is made up, he quickly fills one trolley and another. Drop sheet, hundred and twenty-litre backpack, dry bag, gas stove, travel mug, hammock, bug net, multi-pocket vest, waterproof boots and gaiters, water treatment pills, Leatherman Multi-tool, compass, a month's supply of dehydrated mac and cheese, zip ties.

He opens the pack of zip ties and uses one to attach the third shopping cart to the first two. Then he adds an inflatable kayak, foldable paddle, portage bag, fifty meters of climbing rope, and Coleman fuel lantern. The heavily laden carts have begun to plough furrows into the store's carpeting. He clamps a camping chair under his free arm and removes an inflatable Therm-a-Rest air mattress from a bargain bin using his teeth. The veins in his neck bulge as he maneuvers the wagon train of shopping trolleys to the check-out counters.

"Like a Clydesdale, tilling virgin land," the Frontiersman thinks. "Or an early rancher driving his herd to market."

9

Cart four in the caravan snags on something and stops dead. The plow has hit bedrock. The herd has balked. The Frontiersman swears loudly, the way any ranch hand would. Shoppers who are not ranch hands turn and stare. The Frontiersman ignores them and scans a nearby display stand for chewing tobacco. Finding none, he starts piling his purchases on the check-out counter. He does so roughly. What else to expect from a man of the frontier?

While ceaselessly scanning his surroundings, he catches sight of a new-generation Tilley hat on display behind the cash register. It's classic khaki. The Frontiersman would rather suffer heat stroke than wear blue, olive or burgundy-coloured hats. The khaki Tilley, with its mesh insert for increased ventilation, double chin strap, buoyancy pad and lifetime warranty, holds his gaze with ease.

The Frontiersman grunts at the cashier and thrusts his chin toward the Tilley. "Gimme a couple of those bad boys."

The cashier doesn't love being grunted at but obliges, scans a couple Tilleys and announces the total.

"That'll be four thousand, eight hundred and forty-two dollars and thirty-five cents."

The Frontiersman opens his wallet. It contains three twenty-dollar bills and a taped-together fiver.

He says, "During the gold rush, greedy purveyors like you got rich off the backs of hardworking miners."

The cashier picks up the phone next to the cash register and says, "Security to the check-out counter."

"I'll just take the zip ties," the Frontiersman says.

"That'll be thirteen ninety-nine, plus tax," the cashier says.

In the Frontiersman's mind's eye, a haggard gold miner exchanges a year's worth of gold flakes for a flimsy shovel and crate of hooch. The portly purveyor drums his fat fingers on the counter.

"Supply and demand," the purveyor chirps and sweeps the gold flakes into a drawer bursting with gold dust, nuggets and maybe even ingots.

"Go fuck yourself and your zip ties," says the Frontiersman, now the spokesperson of all miners. Gold, zinc, salt or blood diamond. Of miners dead and alive. Unionized, independent contractors, or enslaved.

"Sir," says the security guard who's suddenly appeared behind the mining spokesperson. "I'm afraid I'm going to have to ask you to leave the store."

The worker's rights activist wheels around, fists clenched. He finds he is looking at the space between the belly button and sternum of a giant. The giant's steady stare indicates his wordy request that the Frontiersman leave the premises is a result of store policy, not politeness or fear of a showdown.

Moments later, the Frontiersman is unlocking his bike from the bike rack. He looks up and down Richmond Road. It's a forest of signs. Lululemon, Pure Kitchen, Baker Street Café, Equator Coffee shop, the Running Room, Pure Yoga. He asks himself where poor people live. Or lived, before the rising cost of membership at Alicia's Bikram yoga forced them to abandon their traditional stomping grounds. Far to the West, just after the kink in Richmond Road where the used car dealerships begin, the

11

Frontiersman can make out the high-rises of Whitehaven and Lincoln Heights. Cheap and nasty housing for recent immigrants to Canada, but the Frontiersman is looking for older poverty. He turns east and pushes his bike past Kitchenalia, a kitchen gadget store selling diminutive prickly pear cacti in plastic pots for one hundred and sixty dollars. Next, he passes Otto's Subaru car dealership, where five-year-old Outbacks with heated seats, backup cameras and the first beads of rust cost thirty grand. He wonders how many ounces of weed his teenage dealer would have to sell to buy a car from Otto. How many night shifts a labourer at Gatineau's Masson paper mill would have to endure to buy a replacement turn signal bulb.

Soon his eastward advance down Richmond Road is rewarded with signs of the neighbourhood's decline. He senses the promise of services other than a pedicure in a nail salon's flickering neon sign. He passes a gas station that doesn't have Tesla charging stations and smells like an oil spill. A vacant lot awaiting the attention of a condo developer collects litter. The Frontiersman pauses at the Real Canadian Superstore supermarket and studies the day's super sale item.

"A gallon of butter-flavoured canola popcorn popping oil for two ninety-nine," he mouths, salivating.

The Frontiersman is no stranger to calorie-intensive processed foods. Like many of his fellow Canadians, he doesn't always have it in him to boil noodles and microwave ready-made pasta sauce. Especially not when ten bucks gets you an extra large pepperoni pizza and a gallon of coke. The thought of all this delicious food worsens the Frontiersman's salivating, and he stops at

House of Pizza for an oily slice of meat-lover's and a Pepsi. The take-out lunch costs him his taped-together fiver.

While waiting for the pedestrian light at Island Park Drive, he espies the blue and white of a St Vincent de Paul's sign. The Frontiersman's perseverance and knowledge of local settlement and displacement patterns have been rewarded, and he sets off with a bounce in his step. He freewheels his bike down the sidewalk and watches it roll half a block or more before scraping to a halt against a parked Subaru.

In front of St Vincent de Paul, he runs the U-lock through his bicycle's rear wheel and frame, then waits politely for someone in a motorized wheelchair to enter the store. The wheelchair operator pushes the handicap open door button marked by a symbol of someone in a wheelchair. The automatic door opens, but not all the way. After several more button pushes, the wheelchair driver goes for broke and floors their means of transport. The wheelchair is electric and, like electric vehicles, enjoys impressive acceleration. But not impressive enough. The wheelchair is halfway into the store when the three-quarter open door reverses direction and becomes entangled in the chair's foot supports. The now immobilized door mechanism groans. The Frontiersman, eager to shop, considers jumping or politely climbing over the wheelchair and its occupant when someone exits the exit door. The Frontiersman slips in through the out door and, with a nod, indicates the door incident to a uniformed security guard. The security guard watches as the wheelchair operator burns rubber trying to reverse out of the door's steely grasp, then wanders into an aisle of summer dresses and disappears.

The Frontiersman makes a beeline for the sports equipment section and finds the mother lode. He lays claim to a faded canvas backpack with a wooden frame. Seven dollars. A rusted but otherwise perfectly presentable hatchet feels right in his palm. He swings at an imaginary bear and is given the stink eye by a mother with three small children. Three dollars. The hatchet, not the children. The Frontiersman drops the hatchet into the backpack and begins to shop in the men's wear aisle. He acquires a pair of short orange shorts, three t-shirts and a plastic rain poncho. Four dollars, the t-shirts are on sale. A peruse of the used shoe rack reveals that his no-nonsense rubber-soled office shoes are peerless. The kitchen utensil bin yields a bread knife with a twelve-inch serrated blade, a rubber cutting board with several dark stains and an enamel mug. Two dollars and fifty cents. No kitchen has ever been renovated for less. He grins, checks for a security camera, and slides a can slash beer opener into his pocket.

"Sixteen-fifty," says the cashier.

While removing a twenty from his wallet, the Frontiersman's peripheral vision catches sight of something shaggy and likely dangerous in a nearby glass display case. His long-dormant hunter-killer instinct is reaching for the hatchet when he realizes it's not a rabid pack of wolves but a hat made of raccoon fur. It has a long yellow and brown striped tail.

"I'll take the hat," he says.

"Fifty cents," says the cashier. "But you'll have to get it yourself. No way I'm touching that."

The Frontiersman slips it on. He lowers the furry brim until he feels like he's peeking out from under the carcass of a freshly slain animal. He lays the tail over his left shoulder, like a ponytail. Then he tries the right shoulder. Not bad either. He tries both shoulders again, this time more slowly and with his chin tucked. The mother of three clears her throat behind him. He changes into his new identity in the restroom. The shorts – 1970s-style tennis shorts – are shorter than he thought. And tighter. He deliberately doesn't choose a t-shirt. Instead, he lays them out on the toilet's water tank and picks one blindly. He only reopens his eyes when he's fully dressed. He accepts what is reflected in the mirror above the sink stoically and with dignity.

"Orange shorts, red t-shirt," he calmly states the facts. "Not ideal, but at least I won't get shot by hunters."

The Frontiersman wonders when hunting season is and concludes he has no clue. He and the bread knife and hatchet will find out soon enough. He shoulders his pack and exits the store. Just in time to see the rear wheel of his bike disappear around the store's far corner. The Frontiersman's response is automatic and primordial. As old as the Old Testament. Maybe older. You steal my camel; I burn your stock of carpets. You enclose the common grazing grounds; we threaten you with universal suffrage. You sell drugs on my corner; I dismember you with a chainsaw.

Instead of tailing the bike thief, he runs in the opposite direction and darts right into the first alley. He might look like Davy Crockett in his new duds, but the Frontiersman is a city boy and prides himself on his knowledge of its

15

thoroughfares and streets, but also back alleys. One of his favourite places to drink beer, for instance, The Carleton, a gloomy watering hole that still serves beer in big bottles, is an easy stagger away. But the Frontiersman isn't in staggering mode and accelerates. The rubber soles of his office shoes adhere to the sidewalk the way the tiny rubbery toes of Amazonian tree frogs stick to the underside of leaves. His thighs, toned from cycling and freed from the friction of pants or shorts that reach below the knee, pump like mighty pistons.

He turns right around the back of the thrift store and, just before rounding the next corner and intercepting the bike thief, lowers his forehead.

Wham! Forehead first into the mother of three he goes. She goes down, blood gushing from her flattened nose. The three terrified children begin to howl. The Frontiersman realizes it's been years since his last First Aid course. Are you supposed to raise the legs or the head? Wrap in a heat blanket or apply ice? What if an attempt to succour the mother would aggravate her injuries? She groans. She might look like a boxer now, but she isn't going to die. The Frontiersman retreats down the alley. He isn't proud of what just happened but knows that sometimes you just gotta move on. It is what it is. No point in looking back. He doesn't and walks into the cinder-block wall at the end of the alley. Stunned, he turns right. Then he goes straight for a block before turning right again. Slightly disoriented, he makes another right and reaches an intersection.

"This should be Spencer," he tells himself.

He looks left. Nothing. He looks right. Less than a block away, there's a police car, ambulance and three distraught children clinging to the gurney containing their mother. The Frontiersman realizes he's nowhere near Spencer. Quickly, he turns away from the crime scene and speed walks down Wellington. There. The faded awning of the Rosemount Public Library. The Frontiersman quickens his pace and jaywalks. Someone honks. His shorts are the subject of several catcalls. He enters the library.

Canadiana

"Please leave your backpack at the door," says a librarian.

The Frontiersman unslings his pack and leaves it by the door.

"Animals are not permitted in the library," the librarian adds and laughs.

The Frontiersman thinks it might be a good idea to give the raccoon hat a break. How many people in Ottawa can be wearing a raccoon hat right now? One? He stuffs the hat into his pack. Now there isn't a single person wearing a raccoon hat in the entire city of Ottawa. He has made the task of anyone looking for an assaulter of mothers with three small children substantially harder.

Under normal circumstances, the Frontiersman never knows where to start in libraries. He simply meanders between the stacks and display tables until something catches his eye. Usually, it's a paperback with an embossed cover featuring a crashing airplane or someone hanging from a burning skyscraper. Over time, he has become uncannily good at judging books by their cover art. But this time is different.

"Canadiana?" he asks someone who is returning books to shelves.

Moments later, he is between stacks that have been artfully decorated with craft paper maple leaves. A localized Indian summer near the letter D has caused leaves to collect on the floor. But the Frontiersman is not afraid of the harbingers of winter. He places a finger on the spine of the first book on the middle shelf and advances slowly down the alphabet. His eyes dart from title to title while scanning the books on the shelves above and below. It's like reading news headlines without actually reading the news. He knows from experience that success is all about finding the right pace. Walk too quickly, and you feel dizzy. Lollygag, and you risk losing sight of the bigger picture.

He stops and pulls *For your Eyes Only* off the shelf. He is dismayed that the book has a subtitle; *Juicy tidbits from Lord Durham's Report of 1839.* Knowing it's difficult to find anything blander than Canadian history, the Frontiersman considers returning the book to the shelf. Instead, he gives the mysterious Lord Durham a chance and flips to the introduction.

If a single event saved Canada from becoming a corrupt banana republic like every single country of Central and South America, or a madhouse of gun-toting libertarian whack jobs like the United States of America, it was Lord Durham's report of 1839 and its recommendations for Upper and Lower Canada.

The Frontiersman yawns but sees that the rest of the book is filled with random quotes. He likes quote books, finds they make for easy, bite-sized reading. He chooses one at random.

"Unifying Upper and Lower Canada into a single province is the perfect opportunity to quietly but effectively and irreversibly bring Francophone Canada to heel. Naturally, we will focus on the advantages of responsible government, bla di bla, but let's not forget what is truly at stake here."

"I knew it," thinks the Frontiersman. He is no stranger to the field of history and chooses another quote.

"At least General Wolfe had the decency to die on the battlefield, unlike General Montcalm, who died the following day in unclear circumstances. What do we really know about the lives of those who are shot in the back?"

Although the Frontiersman doesn't doubt there's merit to looking into the private lives of people who are shot in the back, he returns the book to the shelf.

The next book he pulls from the shelf is *The Settler and his Wife.* He opens the book randomly and reads: *Their lips met with such force that their teeth clashed. The fingers of a trembling hand descended and wrapped themselves around a pulsating and engorged cock.*

The Frontiersman is pleased with this unexpected literary jewel and checks if there's a centrefold. There isn't, but he decides he wants to know more about the settler and the settler's wife and clamps the book beneath his arm. As a precautionary measure, he ensures the title is turned inward, away from the scornful stares of the lost souls perusing the library's self-help and Paulo Coelho sections.

"Pay dirt," he says at the end of the aisle, pulling out a book with a shiny spine. *How to survive the Apocalypse. From making your own toilet paper to eating garbage.. Be prepared.* He runs his finger down the table of contents. *Stocking your deep larder. Designing and decorating your survival retreat. Home security and neutralizing enemies with your bare hands or a hammer.* He sees that the book is in its tenth reprint. This doesn't surprise him. Although not endorsed by Oprah, the Frontiersman guesses the book is compulsory reading for any serious book club. He has a hunch this book will be the manual to his future.

On his way to the check-out desk, he picks up *The Great Traverse: Canoeing across Canada.* He looks at the author's photo and wishes it were his bearded, tanned and ruggedly handsome face looking back at him.

"All books must be returned in a month," the librarian reminds him.

"I'll be sure to do that," the Frontiersman lies.

Spritely Moms and Tall Boys

The Frontiersman dumps the books into his pack and peeks out the door. The police car and ambulance are gone. He sees a Dollar store and a liquor store a few blocks down on the left. He leaves the library and turns left. In the Dollar store, he buys thirty Snickers bars, a carton of no-name cigarettes, a bag of mixed-size zip-ties, bug spray and the latest issue of *Spritely Moms under Twenty.* This earns him a dirty look from the mom over forty at the check-out counter.

"There's no accounting for taste" he reminds her.

The cashier flips open *Spritely Moms* and confronts the Frontiersman with the photograph of a mother who is closer to fifteen than twenty executing a perfect Eiffel Tower position with two black gentlemen.

"That is disgusting," the cashier says. "You should be ashamed."

The Frontiersman strongly disagrees with such a narrow worldview and adds the latest issues of *Beaver Hunt* and *Amazing Juggs* to his purchases.

Twenty-seven dollars later, he exits Dollarama. He wonders why you always spend more than a dollar in a dollar store. He has sixteen dollars left.

"Better make 'em count," he vows and closes in on the liquor store.

His pack has become noticeably heavier. Its wooden frame is creaking. Inside the liquor store it's freezing cold and the Frontiersman puts his raccoon hat back on. The open fridges that chill the store to arctic temperatures are the only thing the Frontiersman doesn't like about liquor stores. The list of things he loves is much longer. Basically endless. For instance, that liquor stores sell not only the advertised liquor but also beer, wine and anything else containing alcohol except rubbing alcohol. Another great thing about Ontario's liquor stores is that provincial and federal taxes are included in the price. That way, when you only have a toonie and decide to invest it in two dollar-a-beer beers, you're spared the embarrassment when the cashier asks you for two dollars plus tax. The Frontiersman can't think of a store he enjoys shopping at more and pauses to pay his respects under a signed portrait of Ontario's buck-a-beer Premier Doug Ford.

He is happily perusing the no-name whiskey section when he sees what can only be a typo. Twenty-four tall boys of Great Lakes Lager for twelve dollars. The Great Lakes Brewery is hardly Anheuser-Busch or Corona, two of the Frontiersman's favourite microbreweries, but typos like this happen once in a lifetime. He moves decisively.

"ID please," says the check-out person.

"But I'm forty," the Frontiersman protests.

"It's for your safety and comfort!" the check-out person reminds him.

The Frontiersman unslings his pack and burrows through its jumbled contents. He finds his wallet and pulls out his driver's license.

"Satisfied?" he asks.

The check-out person provides him with change for the proffered twenty and, with rising inflection, says, "Have a great day." The Frontiersman is loading the beer into his pack and asks whether that was a question or a statement. Whether the check-out person was wishing him a great day or inquiring about his day so far.

"Next," says the check-out person robotically.

"I asked you a question," says the Frontiersman. "My question is whether you asked me a question."

"Security!" the check-out person says, this time without a rising inflection.

What is it with me today? Wonders the Frontiersman.

He slows the packing of beer into the backpack procedure until it resembles an arcane Japanese ceremony of unbearable formality.

"Hurry it up, buddy," says the man in line behind him. The man is holding a six-pack of raspberry and lemon coolers.

"Those for you, Tarzan?" inquires the Frontiersman. "You see?" he adds, turning to the check-out person. "That was a question. A question ends with a rising intonation. If you end all your sentences with rising intonations, all you do is sound like an idiot."

"Sir, I'm going to have to ask you to leave the premises," a uniformed security guard says.

The Frontiersman listens for more upspeak but hears none.

"You betcha," he says and wrestles the top flap of his bulging pack over nearly twelve litres or three point two gallons of Great Lakes Lager. He fastens the flap with a brittle leather strap and swings the backpack onto his back. The beer-laden pack has become massively heavy, and the sudden swinging motion unleashes powerful centrifugal forces. These send the Frontiersman hurtling into the security guard, who in turn ploughs into Tarzan, who crashes into a display of Niagara Peninsula rosé. The display collapses, and broken bottles ooze their sticky pink contents onto the floor.

"Good riddance," reasons the Frontiersman.

He is well-acquainted with the painful consequences of an afternoon spent guzzling rosé from Ontario's Niagara Peninsula. A terroir of terror. Mold-inducing Lake Erie fog banks. Acid rain from Hamilton's heavy industries. General proximity to Buffalo. Add a short and sunless growing season that forces local winemakers to juice their produce with sulphates, oak chips, chemical preservatives, yeast and dextrose, and what can you expect. Not even Premier Ford's benevolent gaze can right these wrongs.

The Frontiersman's pack returns him to the present. While he has been philosophizing about the cons and disadvantages of southern Ontario's climate and soil, the fast-moving backpack has continued circumscribing a wide arc. A beer-filled planet following its God-given orbit. The Frontiersman is in the act of bending down; whether to lend a hand to the fallen security guard or dip a finger into Niagara's finest is unclear when the pack's momentum jerks him upright and hurls him through one of the Liquor store's floor-to-ceiling windows. He bounces off a parked

Subaru, maybe Tarzan's, and lands awkwardly on the sidewalk.

"Thank God I bought cans and not bottles," he thinks, struggling to his feet.

He listens for the telltale hissing sound of a mortally ruptured beer can, hears nothing and thanks his lucky stars. The weight of the pack is now such that the Frontiersman has to lean forward at a forty-five-degree angle just to stay upright. He takes one tiny step forward and then another. And then another and then half a tiny step, and then a full tiny step. Then something shifts in the pack, forcing him to take several large steps back. He manages another minute shuffle forward, then stops and leans against a utility pole sprouting from the sidewalk. He sees he's made it about two feet from the smashed liquor store window and dented Subaru. The Frontiersman has watched enough Westerns and heist movies to know that successful getaways are executed differently.

"C'mon!" he steels himself.

If he can only make it to the end of the block, he can slip from view and be home-free. He grabs a can of Great Lakes Lager through the pack's lid, cracks it and empties it with a few greedy gulps. Lightening his load by four hundred and seventy-three grams plus the weight of the aluminum can doesn't exactly shift the scales of fate, but drinking beer is always fun. He removes two more tall boys, one for each hand, and sets off in the direction of the corner and freedom. The Frontiersman isn't just another oxygen-mask-wearing middle-aged dentist adventurer from Idaho riding to the summit of Mount Everest on the back of some scrawny Sherpa. Oh no. The Frontiersman will forge his own path. Carry his own supplies. And his own beer. Gasping for breath, he eventually reaches the corner and turns left out of view.

He leans the heavy pack against the wall and drains the two tall boys. The air is full of sirens. Suddenly the Frontiersman is overcome by the need to expel a litre and a half of piss-like beer from his straining bladder. He discovers that one advantage of short shorts is that you can simply pull your penis out the bottom of one leg. No need to mess around with the fly. He does just this and relieves himself against the liquor store wall.

If you're going to sell beer, expect to be peed on, the Frontiersman reasons. The beer has not only made his bladder brim over and sharpened his reasoning, but it has also endowed him with superhuman strength, raw courage and zest for action. He sets off immediately, eager to elude his pursuers. As he isn't done peeing, he also urinates down one leg. Not ideal, he tells himself, but at least I'm moving. And at a good pace too. He turns right onto Armstrong, then left onto Hilda.

Traffic

When a police car appears at the end of Hilda, the Frontiersman climbs into the dumpster parked behind Krackers Catering. He discovers a barely touched tray of succulent chicken curry pineapple wraps and helps himself. He has another beer and absentmindedly wipes his curry sauce-covered hands on his legs. His fingers work the sticky orange sauce and pineapple chunks into the hair of his upper thighs, and he is forced to conclude that there aren't only advantages to short shorts. He rinses the sauce and piss off his legs with careful splashes of beer. Then he climbs back out of the dumpster and, after a peek for prowling police cruisers, crosses O'Meara Street. He stays straight on Hilda until reaching Scott Street, a bleak multi-lane thoroughfare.

"Now this is one ugly fucking street," he slurs.

Drunkenness has crept up on him. He eats a Snickers and lights a cigarette. A free newspaper dispenser halfway down the block catches his attention.

The Frontiersman considers it a civic duty to stay informed.

"Democracy dies in the dark," he says ominously and sets off swaying.

After subjecting the dispenser's button and latch opening mechanism to multiple opening strategies, he eventually defeats it by pressing the button and only then lifting the latch. Eager to catch up on current events and neighbourhood issues, he grabs a copy. Then, finding himself holding a glossy real estate prospect masquerading as news, he wraps it around his beer. The mystery of the whereabouts of his cigarette is solved when smoke begins to seep from the real estate prospect dispenser.

Newly determined to stay abreast of society's political discourse, the Frontiersman sets off again. His aim is two-fold: stay unbiased and well-informed and reach the pedestrian crossing at Bayview Station Road. Although his gait is not entirely steady, his nonchalant manner more than makes up for it. No, he knows nothing about any advertisement dispenser that is now burning out of control. He is a tax-paying, vote-casting citizen who is out for a stroll. He takes a sip from his real estate prospect. Unbeknownst to him, beer foam bubbling from the can has begun to soak and weaken the edges of the real estate prospect. When he reaches the Bayview Station pedestrian crossing, things come to a head when an extra large gulp sends a half-page condo ad down his throat. He chokes and coughs, maybe vomits a tiny bit, and clears his throat and spits. Then he waits for the light to change, which takes an eternity. To make the most of the wait, he synchronizes the spitting out of the soaked newsprint with the bleating of the blind person crossing chime.

Beep, spit.

Beep, beep spit spit.

Beep spit.

The pedestrian light changes to green, and the Frontiersman staggers across Scott Street. A car honks. Someone shouts *It's five o'clock somewhere.*

The Frontiersman reaches the far side of Scott Street and, with nothing better to do, waves his middle finger at the backed-up traffic. He lights another cigarette and cracks another beer. He watches as an advanced green light allows a single car to turn left from Bayview Station Road onto Scott Street. The occupants of hundreds of cars waiting to go straight on Scott Street also watch the lone car make the turn. Despite no other vehicle being interested in turning left, an automatic traffic light timer counts down forty-five interminable seconds before turning red. A frustrated motorist honks. The Frontiersman acknowledges their predicament with another supportive wave. Then he does the math. Forty-five wasted seconds times hundreds of waiting cars times one and a half occupants per car equals...incalculable minutes of precious lifetime gone forever.

"Having fun yet?" the Frontiersman yells at no one in particular.

Next, the advance turn signal for traffic turning left from Scott Street onto Bayview Station Road turns green, but the car at the front of the eastbound line doesn't move. It wouldn't surprise the Frontiersman if the car's driver had nodded off or died of old age. At first, no one honks. Then everyone honks. Only the inattentive driver, who is awake and alive, and the next car make it through the intersection before the light turns red again. Next in line are the city buses in their priority lanes. They turn left and right, but their advance is hampered by their lumbering starts and articulated rear-ends. An ambitious bus driver turning onto Scott Street from Bayview Station Road runs a yellow light but is forced to stop mid-intersection for a group of school kids. By the time the school group and bus have exited the intersection, the traffic light has gone from red to green to red again.

"Suckers!" the Frontiersman shouts gleefully.

"Fuck you, you fucking hobo!" the driver of a yellow Mustang shouts.

"I'm an employee of the Federal government!" the Frontiersman shouts back.

What is it with people who drive muscle cars? Were they assholes before they slid behind the wheel of American Muscle, or does being encased in a leather ass gasket and seeing the world through a slit of a tinted windshield turn you into a horizonless brute? The Frontiersman decides to find out and chucks his half-full can of beer at the Mustang. He has always had exceptional hand-eye coordination, and the can disappears into the Mustang's open driver window. Nothing happens. No protest from the Mustang driver. No honking condemnation from the hundreds of other drivers either. The Frontiersman wonders whether this is the silent majority condoning acts of vandalism that target jerk-offs in hot rods. Is the Mustang's silence the result of a brow-beaten bully, or is the driver nipping at what's left of the lager?

"Hey, asshole!" the Frontiersman yells. "You're welcome!"

The pack's straps dig into the Frontiersman's shoulders, and he lightens his load by extracting another beer. He sees that people in the traffic jam have begun filming with their phones. Instinctively the Frontiersman knows that nothing good can come of fame.

Into the Abyss

The Frontiersman takes a step back, a matinée idol disappearing into the satiny folds of a descending curtain and topples backwards into a drainage ditch. The ditch is dry, contains only minimal litter, and the grass on its banks provides shade, padding and camouflage.

"Not too bad," the Frontiersman thinks and observes a spider amble past.

He listens to idling traffic and the insistent beep of the blind-person-crossing signal.

"You and me buddy," he says to the spider.

Something digs into his ribs, and he pulls the Apocalypse guidebook out of his pocket.

"Great compact little format," he thinks and cracks another beer.

Despite Great Lakes Lagers becoming no easier to drink when warm, the Frontiersman chokes down several more gulps.

He flips open the guidebook to *My home is my defensible castle* and begins to read: *If a weekend spent in your depressing suburban home makes you want to shoot yourself and your family, know you are not alone. Recent polls show that people with access to lakeside homes equipped with motorboats and large barbecues are less likely to drink themselves to death in response to the depressing grind of modern life. Yes, the rat race sucks, and drinking is fun, but drinking yourself to death? Get out of Dodge while you still can!*

The Frontiersman considers this bewitching blend of science and philosophy and empties his can of lager. Intrigued, he keeps reading. The following paragraph is a list titled *Choosing your Doomsday bunker.* He scans criteria designed to help readers choose where to make a last stand when society collapses. *Long growing season* is at the top of the list. The Frontiersman eyes the dense foliage that surrounds him. Check. *Rich topsoil.* An unpleasant waft of dog shit informs him that there is no shortage of animal fertilizer. Check. *A lifestyle geared toward self-sufficiency.* The Frontiersman knows he has twenty-nine snickers bars and at least fifteen beers left. He imagines himself slicing Snickers bars into thin wafers and rationing the beer to several daily uncarbonated sips. Check. He wonders if he can hole up in this ditch until it's time to collect his government pension and reads the remaining criteria. *Stay far away from principal thoroughfares. Avoid high-tax environments and all forms of urban planning. Avoid proximity to prisons or large government institutions.*

Bam. Bam. Bam. The coffin containing the dream to live out his days in this green and shady ditch has just had its lid hammered on. Despite the poor lighting in the coffin, the Frontiersman keeps reading and learns why it's essential to stay away from major population centers. *A society in its death throes,* he reads over the rim of another can of lager, *means upheaval, rioting, urban looting, and an everyone-for-*

themselves exodus as cities become flaming infernos. The Frontiersman closes his eyes and relives the traffic jam he just experienced. He takes a cautious sip of lager and adds towering walls of flames and half-melted, errant zombies to the tableau. Finding they don't fundamentally alter the horror of rush hour, he removes them. As if to drive home the point, a frustrated motorist yells *Learn ta fucking drive ya asshole,* presumably at another motorist. Bam. The final nail. A long one. The Frontiersman's dreams of early retirement are now in perfect darkness.

His bladder sounds the full alarm again. He waits to see if it's a false alarm, a the-bladder-who-calls-wolf, but it isn't. Thinking it best to avoid contact with the authorities after recent events, the Frontiersman stays in the ditch, rolls onto his side and forcefully pees up one side of the embankment. Things go well at first, but when his stream's pressure diminishes, he faces a urine flash flood. Instead of panicking, he hauls his pack, Apocalypse guidebook and can of lager deeper into the tall grass. His elbows and nose take turns parting the blades that, from up close, resemble the ferns of an old-growth forest. With the tiniest bit of imagination, the ditch flora could even pass for a regular tropical forest in a faraway country which tigers call home. No allergy attack, grass cuts, or face-to-face encounter with a Bengal tiger. So far, so good. But the Frontiersman knows that all lucky streaks end eventually and readies himself for the worst.

And not a moment too soon. There. Just ahead. A dark hole.

Stealthily he pulls the foot-long bread knife from his pack and clamps it between his teeth. The closer he gets to its dark opening, the bigger it looms. Can it be a nuclear missile silo? The Frontiersman is too concentrated to remember whether Canada has a nuclear arsenal or whether these are ever installed horizontally.

"Only one way to find out," says the alcohol in the Frontiersman's bloodstream.

He rips the pull tab from his lager and lobs the can into the darkness. It clatters.

"Royally mounted Canadian police!" he shouts. "Come up with your hands out. You're surrounded at both ends."

Silence. The Frontiersman crawls into the cool darkness of the culvert. Relief transforms into amazement when he finds an unoccupied mattress. He inches forward and gives it a sniff. Ripe, no doubt, but no more so than his own bedding. He crawls onto the mattress, stuffs the guidebook back into his pack and is instantly asleep.

Along for the Ride

Meanwhile, and unbeknownst to the passed-out Frontiers-man, a nasty weather front is moving down the Ottawa Valley. Somewhere, an Environment Canada meteorologist looks up from his crossword puzzle and studies the dark thermal swirl muscling its way into his computer monitor. The town of Petawawa is first to vanish beneath the storm's vortex, which is soon tearing shingles from roofs in Fort-Coulonge and uprooting trees in Campbell's Bay. After a moment's hesitation, in which the meteorologist decides to saddle someone else with the responsibility of taking action, he reaches for the phone.

"Big one coming," he says into the receiver. "Maybe very big."

The first drops of rain that sprinkle the nation's capital are a welcomed respite from a week of tropical heat and skin-chafing humidity. Ottawans or Ottowonians, or whatever people who live in Ottawa are called, raise their faces to the sky. Children stick out their tongues and try to catch raindrops.

Within minutes the drops of rain have become a torrential downpour. Adults run for cover, and children choke and splutter. The meteorologist leans towards his monitor, detached scientific observation and the lethargy that has its roots in permanent government employment, turning to concern when the unmanned weather station on the roof of the Bayshore Mall reports two inches of rain in as many, or few, minutes. The precipitation pelting the building that houses Canada's Meteorological Services works its way under the window frame and through the wall. Soon a steady rivulet of rainwater tainted with flecks of insulation and decomposing drywall is snaking down the inside of the wall. The meteorologist takes action and moves the backpack containing his lunch and cycling shoes away from the wall.

The Frontiersman is awakened by a clap of thunder and the need to piss. The hand dangling over the edge of the mattress is submerged by the water rushing through the culvert. The mattress is having fits of buoyancy. There's more thunder. It's so loud that the Frontiersman wonders whether the culvert has been hit by lightning and is grateful for Canada's recumbent missile silos. He knows enough about lightning and water to pull his limbs onto the mattress. Now anchorless, it begins to move through the culvert, quickly gathering speed.

This is not the Frontiersman's first rodeo. Weekend camping excursions have been rained out before, and he stays calm and focused. He ensures his wallet is crammed deep into the front pocket of his short shorts. Then he double-checks to see that his pack is watertight. Next, he re-opens the pack's top flap, retrieves a beer, and recloses the flap before opening the beer. He ties the laces of his shoes into double knots. He shakes his head, and water droplets launch from the raccoon fur hat.

By now, the mattress is deep under the city, racing through Ottawa's storm sewer system. Wet to the bone, the Frontiersman is thankful that the city treats rainwater and regular sewage separately. But what about a third, entirely separate system dedicated to handling medium-sized animals that live and then die in cities, and whose shrivelled remains get washed into storm sewers? Or skinnier animals capable of making their own way into a city's sewer, only to get lost and perish from malnutrition or loneliness? Could the two share the same parallel drainage system, or would pipes of varying diameters be required?

These innovations occur to the Frontiersman after a dead and decomposing skunk is washed from an unseen pipe and slaps him in the face. The Frontiersman has put his face into many revolting things, but nothing compares to this. He struggles to remove the skunk from his face, but its claws have become entangled in his raccoon fur hat. The Frontiersman considers ridding himself of the skunk by flinging both it and his new fur hat into the roaring rapids but compromises and swivels the hat so that the skunk is now at the back of his head. This forces him to repeatedly flick the sodden coon tail out of his eyes, like bangs that have grown too long, but he gets used to it and even learns to enjoy the gesture. He experiments with blowing the raccoon bangs to one side but finds that the effort required to move the sodden tail with breath alone leaves him lightheaded.

Suddenly he's in free fall as the storm sewer pipe he was navigating spews its contents into the Ottawa River. With lightning reflexes, he grasps his Lager in one hand

and the mattress, his rig, in the other. Usually a placid river, the heavy downpour has transformed the Ottawa River into class five rapids. Certain sections might be class six or seven. The raging current is heavy with branches, logs and summer cottages built too near its banks. It also boasts discarded shopping carts, car parts, lawn furniture, single-use plastic bags, bottles, straws, stirrers, utensils and cigarette butts. Hoping to subject the participants of this single use plastic picnic organized by the Ottawa Association of smokers to a withering gaze, the Frontiersman shields his eyes and glares upriver.

Then he slams into the river and vanishes beneath its foaming surface. Seconds turn to moments which become slices of a minute before finally becoming an actual minute. Just as we have written him off, the Frontiersman and his mattress, with its two animal figureheads, surge from the depths. Not only is the Frontiersman still at the helm, but he's paddling furiously with the St. Vincent de Paul cutting board. His J-stroke, although skillfully executed, is no match for the river's fury and the situation onboard soon deteriorates. The layers of hair grease, ear wax and dead skin that had impermeabilized the mattress begin to fail, causing it to sit ever lower in the water. The Frontiersman pauses his paddling to take a swig of Great Lakes Lager. He grimaces and wonders whether the Ottawa River is fed by the Great Lakes. His hopes that adding pure Canadian river water might improve its taste have proven false. He closes his eyes and takes another swig. This time it will be a blind tasting. He knows it is the only way to taste without prejudice. He takes time to announce the verdict. When it comes—"Disgusting but potable,"—we can't help but marvel at its judiciousness and equanimity.

Done with the blind tasting, the Frontiersman opens his eyes just in time to stare into the huge intake pipe of the Chaudière Falls hydroelectric plant. Only by arcing his back and holding his hat like a rodeo rider does he manage to stay atop the mattress as it is sucked into the generating station. Although electricity generated with the help of water sounds ecologically friendly, the Frontiersman experiences firsthand that the process involves neither wind chimes nor babbling brooks. On the contrary, inside the hydroelectric plant, it is deafening. The air sizzles and pops with overheated electrons. In the deep roar that seems to be coming from all sides, the Frontiersman doesn't see but senses a life-and-death battle between machines and nature. He thinks it would be a terrible work environment. Then he remembers how low his Francophone colleagues' hydro bills are compared to his own and stares ahead with fresh resolve.

This is not a bad mindset when you find yourself hurtling towards the whirring blades of a twenty-five-megawatt hydro turbine built by General Electric. The Frontiersman flings his can of Lager and Ottawa River water into their flashing midst.

"Take that!" he shouts defiantly.

The can is vaporized.

As his life is about to end, his thoughts wander to beavers and, after a brief but pleasant pause in which he reminisces and tries to remember their many shapes, sizes and owners, to raccoons. Raccoons? he wonders. Although the Frontiersman is puzzled by this varmint association, something in his subconscious commands his hands to hurl the raccoon fur and rotting skunk hat at the rotor blades. The Frontiersman must have read and then forgotten but not entirely forgotten that raccoon hair, and maybe skunk hair too, is extraordinarily dense and, when soaking wet, only becomes denser. This is why wet raccoons look so miserable.

When the twenty-five-megawatt turbine rolled out of General Electric's manufacturing facility in Dearborn, Michigan, five years earlier, its glistening blades were milled to within one one hundredth of one millimetre. By comparison, raccoon hair, regardless if plucked from the black visor around the eyes or the soft-looking tufts of the underbelly, might as well be a fridge. A compact under-the-counter fridge, perhaps, not a double-door behemoth with an in-door ice cube dispenser, but one that nevertheless has space for a small freezer. The turbine's blades snatch the sodden hat from the air and tear at its dense and fibrous mass. Smoke from the turbine's straining crankshaft fills the air. Hampered by tens of thousands of soaking-wet under-the-counter fridges, the mighty blades begin to slow. In a distant control room, an alarm sounds.

"Log jam in turbine three!" a technician shouts and flicks the emergency off switch.

The turbine's still considerable momentum turns the front of the mattress into confetti. The Frontiersman abandons ship by leaping from the stern, but the current pushes him towards the still-spinning blades. He unleashes a deft backstroke that accomplishes nothing and is pulled under by his heavy pack. Disoriented, he opens his eyes underwater. Through the murk and froth, he sees the raccoon tail waving at him. It seems to say *This way, Frontiersman!* The Frontiersman shucks off his pack, wishes it were an underwater sled used by secret service agents instead of a tarpaulin sack strung across a wooden frame and follows it into the maws of the turbine that have shuddered to a halt. The pack and his arms, head and torso slip between two glistening blades. Pass unscathed beneath the guillotine's hovering edge.

Then there's a shift change in the control room. The newcomer flicks off the emergency switch and settles into a plush control room chair with a contented sigh. The giant turbine blades begin to move. The Frontiersman wriggles furiously to escape death's or amputation's grasp. His hips are through, but he feels the blade's metal edge pushing against his upper thighs. The turbine gathers speed, and the Frontiersman is spun around and around. A source of amusement for many, he has always hated amusement park rides. He feels his knees and shins pass over a blade's polished edge, but now his shoes are stuck. The last tufts of coon tail snarling the turbine's crankshaft release their furry grip, and the turbine roars back to life. An instant before it takes off the Frontiersman's business socks, rubber-soled shoes and feet, something happens, and the Frontiersman narrowly escapes an existence without feet. What exactly happened is unclear. Did his pack drift into the nearby overflow channel, where, exposed to the river's full force, it dragged him clear? Did fate intervene? Was it the Frontiersman's guardian angel who riding a performance-enhanced Seabob chariot, carried the day? Or did the author run out of ideas and clumsily use a solve-all plot device? Certain is only that the river's icy thrust instantly chills the remaining Lagers to a pleasant temperature.

The Frontiersman, entangled in his pack but minus his raccoon hat, ricochets along a giant pipe and, moments later, is ejected from the power station. He barely has time to gasp for air when he plunges into the rapids that rage under the Eddy Street bridge. Pernicious eddies suck him under, but each time he fights or doggy paddles his way back to the surface. The river is treacherous, but it is also shallow and rocky, and the Frontiersman is pummeled against granite outcroppings and regular round river stones that hurt no less for having nice rounded edges. A Schwinn bicycle that is rusted beyond repair flashes past. The shadow of another Bridge passes overhead. The Frontiersman clings to his pack and to life. And to the faint hope that his cigarettes have somehow made it through this ordeal. Just as the analgesic effect and liquid courage of the Lager wears off once and for all, he washes aground. In a heart-wrenching scene involving crawling and the Frontiersman using his front teeth to drag himself away from the river, he inches ashore. Evolutionary cycles are quicker. Then his last pint of strength fizzles, and he passes out.

Wrap-Around Sunglasses

When the Frontiersman regains his senses, it is warm and sunny. The clear blue sky holds no trace of the sudden storm that nearly cost him his life.

"My ciggies!" he thinks, suddenly panicked.

IIe scrambles to his feet and dumps the contents of his pack on the grass. It's a pitiful sight. The once impeccable bread knife is now flecked with surface oxidation. The hatchet, already rusted, appears unchanged at first glance but has undoubtedly rusted a little more. The spare t-shirts and poncho are soaked and spotted with raccoon hair. The Frontiersman decides then and there that he will wear these hairs proudly. An homage to the courageous beast that gave its life twice to save him. The enamel mug is half full. He is unsure if with Great Lakes Lager or Ottawa River water. He sips but can't tell the difference. His extensive library of books and specialty magazines is not unscathed, and he spreads them out in the grass to dry, taking care to unfold the centrefolds and weigh them down with stones. His larder is soaking wet but complete. He opens the wrapper of a Snickers bar, pours out the water, and takes a bite. Delicious. He wonders what secret ingredients make this the best chocolate bar in the world. He counts twelve cans of lager, some full, others in varying states of emptiness. Carbonation hisses from at least one punctured can. Does carbonation contain methane? The Frontiersman doesn't know, but he's damned if he's going to contribute to warming the earth's atmosphere. He opens the damaged cans and empties them. Down his throat. The cigarettes are another story. One of utter desolation. He gingerly opens the water-logged packs and lays the cigarettes out to dry. Wounded soldiers, convalescing on the grounds of a stately manor that happened to be built on the edge of a great battleground. Or maybe the battle erupted nearby and spilled without permission into its extensive English Garden. Regardless, the Frontiersman knows that not every cigarette will make it. Some of their wounds are simply too terrible. The thought of triage is unbearable.

If the Frontiersman were a regular tourist and not a solitary Red Cross figure fighting to save the lives of others, he'd have noticed that he washed up on the riverside lawn of the Canadian Museum of History. As it's a beautiful sunny day, the grass expanses are packed with families enjoying picnics.

The father of one such family saunters over.

"How much for a cigarette?"

"Dime," says the Frontiersman.

The father hands the Frontiersman a dime and admires his collection of smut while dragging heavily at the damp cigarette.

"Quite the yard sale," the father says.

The Frontiersman recalls the Apocalypse guidebook's insistence on the importance of barter.

"Your choice of magazine in exchange for your wife's baseball hat," says the hatless Frontiersman.

The father looks at his wife who is wearing a baseball hat that reads *Rainbows forever.*

"But it's pink," says the father.

"So is that," says the Frontiersman pointing at one of the many pink things in the centrefold of *Beaver Hunt.*

A deal is struck. Two individuals motivated by their free will, or is it wills because there are two of them, or willies, engaging in honest commerce. Their intention to hold up their end of the bargain sealed with a manly handshake.

Two policemen on bikes cut across the lawn from the riverside bike path and stop in front of the yard sale.

"No camping," says the cop wearing the wrap-around sunglasses that are preferred by professional athletes, people who would like to pass as professional athletes or regular assholes.

"I'm not camping," explains the Frontiersman. "I nearly drowned in the river and am drying out my stuff. I'll be gone in an hour."

Sunglasses issues him a seventy-five dollar fine for swimming in a no-swimming zone.

The Frontiersman protests. He hadn't chosen to swim here. He was minding his business and napping in a ditch when yesterday's storm washed him into the river.

"I barely avoided being turned into tartar in the hydroelectric dam," the Frontiersman concludes.

The cops exchange a look. Sunglasses issues the Frontiersman a one hundred and fifty dollar fine for trespassing on the property of Hydro Quebec. The

Frontiersman recognizes the abuse of petty authority when he sees it and looks straight at Sunglasses to let him know that he knows. His gaze, just and unwavering, is reflected back at him by the wrap-around's reflective lenses. He knows you have to retreat from certain battles to win the war. This battle is lost. He raises his hands.

"I'm clearing out," he says and begins stuffing his belongings into his pack.

"Are you threatening us?" Sunglasses clambers off his bike.

"No sir, officer," the Frontiersman says, carefully stowing wet cigarettes in the side pockets of his pack. "Gimme a minute, and I'll be on my way."

Sunglasses, his police duty belt and its many accoutrements breach the Frontiersman's personal space.

"Put your hands above your head," Sunglasses orders. "Now!"

The last twelve hours of the Frontiersman's life haven't been a cakewalk, and he is functioning well below his regular cognitive potential. When he pulls his hands from his pack to hold them above his head, one holds the bread knife and the other the hatchet. Both police officers reach for their sidearms. Sunglasses shouts at him to lower his hands. The Frontiersman complies instantly and throws down his arms. The grip of the hatchet has been rendered slimy and slippery by its trip through the storm sewers and slips from the Frontiersman's descending hand. It spins through the air and cleaves deeply into the head of Sunglasses' sidekick. Blood arcs from the gaping cranial wound. The Frontiersman panics and raises his hands, this time in surrender. The serrated bread knife he is holding also surrenders. Its foot-long blade slashes through the air and slices into Sunglasses' neck. Blood geysers into the air. Sunglasses falls to his knees, head hanging by a thread. Picnicking families scream and scatter. The Frontiersman, too shell-shocked to think clearly or think at all, shoulders his pack and scatters with them.

Shit coloured plywood boxes

Is the Frontiersman a cold-blooded killer hoping to benefit from the anonymity of large crowds? Is he one of those people who jog while wearing weighted vests, in his case a heavy backpack? Or is he innocent and confused, afraid and running scared? Would a crime scene reenactment by trained professionals reveal that the deaths of the two bicycle-mounted police officers were the tragic result of a misunderstanding? Were the cops speaking French? Québécois? Joual? If so, was what they said comprehensible to an anglophone government employee with years of costly bilingual training?

Hard to say. Right now, things are too chaotic. The Frontiersman pulls down the rainbow-coloured brim of his new baseball cap and covers the remaining distance to the Champlain Yacht Club parking lot in a hunched-over sprint. Here he is nearly run over by a speeding Subaru. Heated steering wheel, anti-rust undercoating updated yearly, Thule roof box, bicycle rack, also by Thule. The works. The Subaru reaches the boom barrier at the exit of the lot, but unlike in action movies, it doesn't ram through but slows and stops. Peeking from between cars, the Frontiersman watches as the front seat occupants frantically rummage for a credit card. A credit card is jammed into the card reader.

The boom rises, and the Subaru accelerates out of the lot. Just before it is lost from view, the Frontiersman can be seen clinging to its bike rack. The credit card abandoned in the card reader glints darkly in his hand.

The horror of seeing two badge and short-wearing police officers get hacked to pieces is fresh on the mind of whoever is driving. The Subaru races down Laurier Street as though trying to escape death itself. This is foolish, of course. Death has no need to run or break the speed limit. It simply floats along, its hooded gown barely touching the ground, effortlessly keeping abreast of whoever is trying to cheat it. The Subaru careens left on Sacred Heart Boulevard, then accelerates up the on-ramp of eastbound highway fifty. The Frontiersman crouches low on the bike rack but finds it hard to get comfortable. He wonders how bicycles manage. As the Subaru races past the Gatineau city limit sign, the Frontiersman risks a peek over the roof and is rewarded with a bug impact to the right eye. Using only his left eye, he takes in his surroundings.

Taupe suburbs as far as his left eye can see. Hundreds of thousands of plywood boxes coated in shit-coloured vinyl siding are confined by listing pressure-treated wood fences. Upper floors with too-small, off-centred windows stare at the blighted landscape like retarded cyclopses. Ground floor facades feature Greek columns, cramped front porches and oversize recycling bins. Picture windows with fake granite trim are barricaded by California blinds and giant flatscreen televisions. The proportion of these boxes intended for human habitation is dwarfed by that dedicated to cars. The Frontiersman counts two, three and even a six-car garage. Shopping plazas, gas stations and car dealerships round out these brand-new communities. The Frontiersman refuses to witness such ugliness and shuts his left eye in protest.

The car behind the Subaru begins to honk. The Frontiersman re-opens his left eye and sees it is also flashing its high beams. The Frontiersman mouths *I know that there's no seat belt back here,* but it soon becomes apparent he is not the intended recipient of the attention-getting tactics. The Frontiersman realizes he can't continue to hide in plain sight and, pushing off from the bike rack with his reliable rubber-soled shoes, propels himself onto the Thule roof box. Using the bloodstained bread knife, he saws through the box's hard plastic lid and climbs in.

"Much better," he thinks, enjoying the view through his very own sunroof.

Despite the day's tragic events and the city-wide manhunt for a cop killer, the weather is perfect, and the sky is dotted with fluffy clouds. The Frontiersman, still reeling from the sudden turn his life has taken, searches the clouds for faces or objects or an explanation. A watering can, a unicorn, a smiley face, anything. Failing, he tries and does not succeed in lighting a cigarette. A beer can digs into his back but contort himself as he may; he simply can't reach it. He stops struggling and is nodding off when the Subaru slows and turns down an off-ramp. After an eternity at a traffic light, it sets off again. Several turns and a parking maneuver that hints at an obsessive compulsive disorder later, the Subaru comes to a halt, and its occupants get out.

"Anyone up for a milkshake?" a man's voice asks.

The tone of forced gaiety is intended to shift the family's focus from gory dismemberment back to a thrill-filled weekend outing. The ruse works. Children's voices affirm their desire for a milkshake. Ones with minced M&M's and extra caramel sauce. The voices recede and vanish.

If You Can't Beat 'Em, Join 'Em

The Frontiersman peers out his sunroof and sees he's in a parking lot lined with big box stores. There's a Canadian Tire, Walmart, Best Buy, the Brick, Office Depot, Giant Tiger and several all-you-can-eat buffets. A Videotron Superclub, Econofitness gym, Costco, formerly family-run Greek restaurant that has gone out of business, Value Village, second Giant Tiger and Ford dealership are also present. Everything anyone could need. Or want. Or think they need or want. Or be made to think they need and want.

The Frontiersman is many things, but a party pooper he is not.

"If you can't beat 'em, join 'em," he says, clambering down from the Subaru.

With fingertips still shrivelled from his recent white-water rafting expedition, he traces the reassuring outline of the credit card through the material of his shorts. After what he has begun to think of as *The unfortunate incident of the slippery hand,* he guesses it's best to change his appearance. He sets off diagonally across the continent-sized parking lot and, fifteen sweaty minutes later, pushes into Value Village. He pauses at the entrance and inhales deeply. The unique perfume of pre-owned, heavily discounted junk brimming with potential is a smell he loves. The Frontiersman's love of boundless possibilities is matched only by his hatred for shopping, so he randomly selects several two-piece jogging outfits from the men's leisure wear section. The good thing about jogging pantsuits, he knows, is that they always fit, unlike business suits.

In the sporting goods section, he scores rubber boots. He asks a passing employee for a large fish tank or a rubber boot testing facility but is told there isn't one.

Next, he pulls an imitation Tilley hat from a rack that contains everything from wool hats to dog walking leashes to long-haired wigs. On a hunch, he selects two wigs. One has shoulder-length glossy brown curls. The other wig has a significant bald spot and an orangey fringe. It strikes him as odd that someone would want a wig with a bald spot surrounded by greasy strands, but who is he to judge. Two fifty-cent pairs of sunglasses later, he is at the check-out.

"Six dollars even," says the cashier.

"That's crazy," says the Frontiersman. "How often is the total an even number?"

"Uh-huh," says the cashier.

The Frontiersman hands the cashier his new credit card. It is a black Amex Centurion. While the cashier waits for the card reader to do its thing, the Frontiersman fiddles with the pen that is attached to the cash register by a string.

"No need to sign," the cashier says. "Amex Centurions have a minimum credit limit of a million."

The cashier, who has clearly worked at stores other than Value Village, hands back the credit card and looks straight at the Frontiersman.

"Here's your card Mister…."

The three dots hang in the air menacingly. The fourth dot is the period that marks the end of the cashier's incomplete sentence.

"My name's confidential," says the Frontiersman.

"Your name is written on the front of the card," says the cashier.

The Frontiersman looks at the card. Indeed. Leviathan Ezekiel. Great name. Even if he's not sure which is the first name.

"You sure this is your credit card, Mr. Ezekiel?" the cashier's hand has begun to move toward the cashier's phone.

"Can I add a tip with this bad boy?" The Frontiersman waves around the credit card with what he hopes is the nonchalance of an experienced shopper. "In appreciation for the excellent service I've received in this world-class establishment?"

The cashier deftly swipes the card and hands Leviathan the card reader. The Frontiersman enters one thousand dollars and presses the green button. The terminal instantly spits out a receipt. Spending other people's money has always been easy, but this is crazy.

After a bathroom stop to change into his jogging outfit and bald wig, the Frontiersman is back in the parking lot. Concrete wastelands lined with stores selling useless garbage hold an entirely different appeal to Amex Centurion card-holders.

The Frontiersman enters a Circle-K convenience store and purchases a super-sized Slurpee and two hundred and fifty dollars worth of beef jerky. Back on the tarmac, he shields his eyes. Sunlight reflecting off car windshields shines into his eyes like a thousand tiny rectangular suns. He slips on a pair of fifty-cent sunglasses and is surprised by how far he can see. They must be prescription sunglasses. The Frontiersman is pleased with this unexpected windfall. A flashing sign at the far side of the parking lot catches his eye.

"All-you-can-eat lunch buffet," he says, reading aloud.

He realizes he is famished. How long ago was that nasty slice of pizza? Or those wraps he scavenged from the dumpster? Too long. He begins his traverse of the parking lot but is stopped halfway by a Slurpee-induced brain freeze. He leans against a car and waits for the sensation of a life-ending aneurysm to pass. When it does, he kicks the remaining Slurpee under a nearby vehicle. His rubber boots keep his feet from getting wet. The sun beating on his rubber bald spot has soon thawed the last of the brain freeze, and by the time he arrives at Club Pigale, the gentleman's cabaret club with the lunch special, he's his regular self again.

Old Bald Pervert

"No vagrants," says the bouncer at the door of Club Pigale. Then switching to his native Quebecois, he adds, "*Décriss espèce d'ostie de colon.*"

"Décriss this, p'tit criss," the Frontiersman says brandishing the Amex Centurion. He always aced the government's French language tests.

The bouncer carries the Frontiersman's pack into the club, where the lighting is low and the standards lower.

"Bucket o' wangs and a Corona!" the Frontiersman shouts at a tired-looking woman leaning against a pole.

She points a nicotine-stained finger in the direction of the buffet.

"Wangs and Poon Tang," the Frontiersman says dreamily, listing two of his favourite food groups.

On his way to the buffet, he orders four bourbons. The sparse and gelatinous spread would be a disappointment for anyone who had eaten more than a soggy Snickers and dumpstered curry wraps in the past twenty-four hours, but the Frontiersman has never seen a finer smorgasbord. He piles deep-fried wanton balls onto a bed of barely warm instant mashed potatoes, dumps a bowl of artificial onion flakes on top and eats the first plate standing at the buffet.

He carries his second course—microwaved broccoli, six cheese-filled hot dogs and celery sticks laden with garlic mayonnaise—back to his table and downs two bourbons.

"Let's see what you got!" he yells at the dancer, who begins to rub her ass against the pole.

The Frontiersman orders a bottle of champagne and lights a cigarette. A voice over a loudspeaker tells him to put out the cigarette. He finishes the remaining whiskeys and weaves his way back to the dessert table.

"Living in a sewage gully one moment and in the lap of luxury the next," he says introspectively and wonders what curve ball fate will throw his way next. Will it be an underarm softball pitch? A fast knuckleball?

A firm believer that fruit does not constitute dessert, the Frontiersman focuses on selecting starches, fats and sugars. He espies a heap of Nanaimo bars and remembers reading that a single one contains enough calories to sustain an adult for several days. He carries the entire tray back to his table. By the time he has washed down three, the champagne is empty. He orders another bottle.

"Dom Perignon," he shouts at the departing waitress. "Biggest you got."

The manager appears, wishes him a great day and sets an ashtray on the table.

"How do I get a dance?" the Frontiersman asks. "Not with you," he clarifies. The manager is potbellied, five-foot-one and wears rings and a thin ponytail.

"With her." The Frontiersman points at a young dancer waiting her turn near the exit door.

"That's my daughter," the manager says. "I'm driving her to Girl Guides."

The Frontiersman knows there's one way and one way only through life, which is forward.

"What about her?" He points at a nearby woman wearing a skintight leopard skin dress and enormous collagen-enhanced lips.

"That's my wife," the manager says tightly.

"Family-run business," the Frontiersman says. "I like it. Nice homey feel."

The waitress appears with an ice bucket containing a triple Magnum of Dom Perignon Rose Gold. Her eyes dart to the manager, who nods imperceptibly. Or almost imperceptibly. The years the Frontiersman has spent staring at the wall clock in his cubicle, willing it forward, have made him an astute observer. Have taught him to break down the movement of the second hand into several distinct phases: The optimistic lurch forward as it accelerates across time. The agonizing torquing of the arm as time quashes its youthful advance. Then the rocking back and forth and the licking of wounds as it plots its next desperate escape. The waitress's glance and owner's nod tell the Frontiersman that the triple magnum doesn't contain Dom Perignon Rose Gold. That it's nothing but an old bottle filled with cheap sparkling wine that gets trotted out to dupe drunken patrons. An advocate of honesty, the Frontiersman shares his thoughts with the manager.

"First, you insult my family and now my establishment?" The manager has raised his voice.

The bouncer, still seething at being treated like a bellhop, is inbound. The Frontiersman gauges that he has just enough time to set things straight.

Addressing the manager, he says: "Your daughter's hot, your wife's a six, and you're a crook. Lunch and drinks are on you, or I call the cops."

Before the manager can reply, the bouncer, a man of action, throws a haymaker at the Frontiersman. He also slips on a French fry that's been trodden into the carpet, and as he's wearing leather-soled Gino loafers instead of sturdy anti-slip shoes with good ankle support, he pitches forward. His massive fist connects squarely with the wife's face. Her humongous pout explodes in a spray of liquefied gelatin.

"Maman!" the daughter cries in a delightful French accent and rushes towards her fallen mother.

The Frontiersman is mesmerized by the sight of the daughter crossing the bar. Is she moving in slow motion, or is his brain savouring the moment? Lithe limbs, narrow hips, unblemished skin. Her mouth is frozen in that half-open position that French lips assume when they make the sound mɑ. The Frontiersman wishes he were a vowel or a mother. Her mother.

But he knows it's too late for this. Instead, he wrestles the four-and-a-half litre bottle to his lips. A geyser of raspberry-flavoured sparkling wine erupts from the bottle and blinds the Frontiersman. He tumbles backwards, narrowly avoiding the bouncer's second roundhouse. Not finding its intended target, the sucker punch connects with the manager's cheek. Face down in a puddle of raspberry bubbly, the Frontiersman's groping hands find the neck of a bottle. He drains it reflexively, then uses it to club the bouncer. The unmistakable burn of *Calle Veinte Tres* scorches his throat, and he wonders why it never occurs to him to order tequila with lunch. He feels a profound respect for people who do. Then he's back on his feet, wiping the carbonated plonk from his eyes and taking stock of the situation. The bouncer, manager and wife are out for the count. The daughter, the goddess-in-training, the almost-woman who could stay by his side forever and tend to him in old age, is crouching next to her knocked-out mother.

"Come!" the Frontiersman says, beckoning her over. "We'll leave now. It's not too late."

The daughter tells him to fuck off.

The Frontiersman has read that certain phases of an adolescent's life can be difficult and that during these periods, they can behave worse than untrained circus animals, which makes them hard to love. To his credit, the Frontiersman doesn't hesitate. He tells the daughter that he'll wait for her. That he'll be there when he needs her. That he doesn't know where he's going or when he'll be back, but that she can count on him. At least spiritually.

He breaks the silence by taking another swig from the triple magnum. Wave-size gulps pour down his front, but he manages to keep them out of his eyes and nose this time. He even manages to divert some into his mouth. He offers the daughter a sip, but she grimaces in disgust. Or does she smile? He winks at her. She shows him the screen of her phone. He squints and sees the numbers nine one one. He doesn't recognize the area code.

"Club Pigale," the daughter says into the phone. "Armed robbery. Old bald pervert. I think he's going to hurt me."

Old? Pervert? The Frontiersman is speechless. The insinuations sting. And sober him up.

"Ingrate!" he shouts at her. It's a terrible thing to say to a woman, but his feelings are hurt, and what does he care if she throws the rest of her life away. "Strumpet!" Hell hath no fury like a man rejected.

He shoulders his pack and pushes through a rear fire exit.

No Fun Shoes

Emerging onto the mall's scorching parking lot after his mostly pleasant time in the dimly lit Club Pigale is like being born. The Frontiersman's is a difficult and traumatic birth. He instantly regrets his last greedy gulps of raspberry wine and briefly considers but just as quickly discards the option of assuming a fetal position. He knows the chances of someone raising him to a pair of doughy maternal breasts are slim. Distant sirens grow less distant. He sets off across the parking lot.

The daughter's words ring in his ears. Bald, old, pervert. Did feminine intuition permit her to see through him? To discover and condemn facets of his character that are unknown even to him? He works his way down the list. Bald. He ditches the tonsure wig and pulls on the brunette one. Old? Who is she to judge? Was she even legal? He decides that age, except maybe the age of consent, is relative. A pervert? He wonders whether perversion is subjective. Can it be measured? Not by puritanical and narrow-minded moral guardians who make laws and willfully ignore life's darker and more complex pleasures, but by laxist psychoanalysts willing to blame all human frailty on injustices suffered in past existences. The Frontiersman wonders where he fits on the perv scale.

"Lower quartile," he lies to himself.

A police cruiser rockets into the parking lot and screeches to a halt in front of Club Pigale. The Frontiersman drops out of sight and crawls under a parked car. The apocalypse guidebook slips from his pack and falls open in front of him. He reads *How to choose your get-out-of-Dodge vehicle.*

The Frontiersman has never owned anything larger than a bus pass. And a bicycle that was recently stolen. This abstinence from vehicle ownership is not due to an ecological sense of responsibility or not being licensed to drive but because no apartment he has ever rented has come with a parking spot. At least not one big enough for the pickup truck he's always dreamed of. His eyes wander to the Ford dealership. His fingers close around the black Amex Centurion. Would he choose extra thick rubber floor mats? Splurge on a winch and gun rack? Are gun racks even sold this close to Ottawa?

The giddiness he experiences in the antechamber of consumption distracts the Frontiersman, and he reads about Getting out of Dodge but doesn't comprehend. His heart sinks when he rereads the passage on choosing the perfect ride for the apocalypse. The apocalypse doesn't share his closeted admiration for North America's best-selling passenger vehicle. His hunger for knowledge forces him to re-re-read. He does so out loud, his voice echoing under the car. The apocalypse is explicit. *Do not even think of buying a flashy but poorly made and wildly fuel-inefficient pickup truck. Ford, Dodge, Chevrolet, GMC. They are all pieces of shit hiding beneath layers of plastic chrome. You'll break down or run out of gas way before escaping the looting and murdering zombie hordes.*

The Frontiersman knows just as well as the marketing departments of this world that buying stuff is half the fun. Maybe even more than half. Because how much fun is moving whatever piece of junk you just bought to your basement or garage once the novelty has worn off? The responsibilities of ownership, maintenance, keeping the warranty booklets organized or having to buy replacement widgets when your plastic acquisition breaks are zero fun. The Frontiersman wonders whether this means that the act of buying something should be followed by throwing whatever you just bought directly into the garbage. Grudgingly he reads on.

What you're looking for is a 1970s Buick Estate station wagon. Easy to maintain, big block engine to ram stuff out the way and lots of room for guns, ammo, protein bars, camouflage nets, spare tires and cases of beer or corn-based liquor. In the case of a nuclear attack and electromagnetic radiation, your station wagon will still start. Unlike the finicky gadget-ridden Subarus of this world.

Only now does the Frontiersman realize he'd ditched his Subaru ride in the nick of time. He tries not to imagine being cooked alive in a plastic roof box by an atomic blast.

"What are you doing under my car?" a voice inquires.

The Frontiersman looks up from his reading and sees a pair of no-fun shoes. He rolls over to introduce himself but gets wedged between the parking lot and the car's exhaust pipe.

"Reading," he shouts. There is no shame in telling the truth.

"I'm calling the cops," the no-fun shoes say.

The Frontiersman takes a closer look at his interlocutors. They aren't even shoes. They are sturdy rubber sandals lashed to a pair of feet with multiple Velcro straps. He has never seen anything so ugly.

"No need," the Frontiersman says, wiggling out from under the car. "Just go to Pigale's. You'll find the cops there."

Now that he is standing and looking out over the sea of parked vehicles, the Frontiersman sees the heads of numerous police officers weaving between the cars. What he doesn't see is a single Buick Estate station wagon. He goes into a crouch, and several of his long locks get tangled in the sandals' Velcro straps. The Frontiersman and the sandal-wearer spend several awkward minutes kneeling head to head as they untangle their belongings. The Frontiersman offers some beef jerky as compensation for the hassle, but his peace offering is turned down. Some relationships were simply not meant to be, and the Frontiersman vanishes in the maze of automobiles.

"Old, bald, pervert." The walkie-talkie on a nearby policeman's belt summarizes the situation. "Be on the lookout for a bald Caucasian male between late-middle age and the home stretch. He's a dangerous pervert whose idea of lunch is a titty bar buffet."

"Could be anyone," the fifty-something, bald police officer with memberships at various local strip clubs mutters darkly. "Could be me."

Perturbed that dispatch is now profiling people based on his hobbies, the fifty-something officer stumbles over a curb and accidentally fires his weapon. Several colleagues return friendly fire. There are screams and panic as terrified shoppers laden with plastic goods and huge soft drink containers seek cover.

Biggest Wheels You Got

The situation is spiralling out of control. The noose is being pulled tight. But the Frontiersman remains calm in the face of adversity and strides confidently into the air-conditioned atrium of the Ford dealership. Once inside, he stands still, breathing deeply. Unlike Value Village's aroma of undiscovered treasures, a secondhand ashtray in the shape of a black panther, say, the dealership smells pungently of fresh rubber and recently topped-up engine lubricants. It is the smell of order. Of viscous black goo that was wasting away beneath the earth's surface until it was rescued and turned into liquid gold. Gold that powers humanity's basic needs. Like portable, softly-purring electric generators. Or those extra thick rubber floor mats the Frontiersman dreams of. The powerwasher-resistant ones. Or fleece-lined fly fishing waders. Or tent pegs sold in packs not of five but of twenty. Or super absorbent paper towels and hundred-piece ratchet sets made by DeWalt. Or even...

"Sir, we're closed," says an anxious-looking man who has taken cover behind the reception desk.

"No, you're not," says the Frontiersman, raising his voice to be heard over the gunfight in the parking lot.

He slaps the Amex Centurion on the faux marble melamine reception, shakes out his long brown curls and dumps his pack onto a nearby chair.

"Got any Ford Raptors?" the Frontiersman inquires airily? "King cab. Four-wheel drive. Biggest wheels you got."

The dealership re-opens. The no longer anxious man who is, in fact, a salesperson is well acquainted with Amex Centurions. He assures the Frontiersman that Raptor models are available. After typing on his keyboard, he turns the screen to face the Frontiersman.

"Ever heard of the Shelby Raptor?"

The Frontiersman once met a girl in a bar named Shelby. But that's the extent of his knowledge.

"My dad used to own one," the Frontiersman lies. "Way back when. Great ride."

The salesperson wonders whether way back when refers to three years ago when Ford first began stuffing massive engines into under-engineered pickup trucks. Not one to harp on genealogy, he starts rattling off specs.

"Seven-hundred-plus horsepower, dual exhaust pipes, two-toned leather seats."

A police cruiser crawls past the dealership and interrupts the sales pitch. The salesperson gives the officer behind the wheel a friendly thumbs up. All good here; no need to stop. The cruiser inches out of sight.

When the salesperson looks back across the reception desk, the Frontiersman has vanished.

"Over here," says the Frontiersman, who is standing between a potted fern and a rack of pamphlets.

The salesperson finds his focus again. "Heated coffee cup holder. Your java will never get cold."

He squints at the Frontiersman, who has opened his hand and is mouthing what appears to be *I'll take five.*

The salesperson's calculator appears out of nowhere. No ballet ensemble or even Irish dance troupe can match the dance his fingers perform on its buttons.

"That'll be six hundred and thirty-seven thousand, nine hundred and twenty dollars," the salesperson says breezily.

"Do you deliver?" the Frontiersman whispers from the underbrush.

The dealership will deliver.

Using the pamphlet rack as an ugly but mobile room dividing screen, the Frontiersman makes his way to a nearby map of Eastern Canada. The salesperson follows. Outside, an armoured truck with SWAT written on the side races past.

"Let's see," the Frontiersman says.

He can't remember the last time he looked at a map of Eastern Canada.

"Deliver one here. One here. One here and one…," his finger hovers over an area the size of continental Europe.

"Here. Right here." The Frontiersman's finger descends on Fermont, Quebec, one thousand kilometres north of Quebec City, population two thousand and change, with finality.

The Frontiersman and his finger are following the lead of an ancient spirit hound. One that has been muzzled for too long. The salesperson makes note of the desired delivery locations that ascend the St. Lawrence River before veering left into Labrador and to places where there aren't roads, much less Ford dealerships.

"And Shelby number five?" the salesperson inquires.

The Frontiersman jabs his finger at the map without looking. "Right here is where I want that last baby."

The salesperson squints and reads *Pangnirtung*, a dying hamlet on Baffin Island.

"Will Iqaluit do?"

The Frontiersman has never heard of Iqaluit but gives his assent.

The calculator is back under the salesperson's dexterous fingers.

"Add your federal and provincial taxes and shipping," he mutters.

He steals a glance at the Frontiersman, who is either staring into the parking lot or his unknown future. The salesperson adds a few zeros.

"One point two mil," he announces.

The Frontiersman and salesperson return to the reception desk where the credit card terminal lives. Mr. Ezekiel's card is swiped, the charge is approved, and papers are signed. The Frontiersman serves himself a mouthful of water in a paper cone from the water dispenser. Strangely he feels no elation at having fulfilled a childhood dream five times. This can't be said for the salesperson who has just become the salesperson of the decade. The din of circling police helicopters snaps the Frontiersman from his funk. He teases his brown bangs, slips on his second pair of Value Village sunglasses, gives the salesperson an I'm-counting-on-you stare, and sidles out a side door. Cars in the parking lot have thinned out and have been replaced with police cruisers and news channel vehicles.

"Not good," thinks the Frontiersman.

His pack feels like a bullseye. Even if police weren't looking for a cop killer with an antique burlap backpack, anyone able to carry their worldly belongings on their shoulders in this haven of pathological consumption would look suspicious. The Frontiersman slips off the pack and tries pulling it behind him like a wheelie suitcase. But the pack may have been manufactured before wheels were invented, and its wooden frame bumps and scrapes along the pavement. The Frontiersman shoulders it and does his best to conceal it under his brunette mane. His eyes scan his surroundings for shelter. There! Bingo! The six-foot brunette hunchback strikes a beeline.

The Ur-Predator

"I-74," A booming voice announces.

The Frontiersman takes a seat at the back of the hall and scans the handful of cards he purchased at the door. His bingo dabber hovers but doesn't descend.

"N-25," the voice continues.

Dab. Dab.

"O-43"

Dab. Dab. Dab.

Dab.

The Frontiersman feels the tension ebb from his shoulders. The octogenarian player to his right is not only relaxed but asleep. Is the one face down across from him sleeping forever? The Frontiersman minds his own business.

"B-57"

Dab. Dab. Dab. Dab. Dab.

His pulse quickens. The Frontiersman is no poker face, but he's not afraid to win either.

"G-13"

Dab. Dab. Dab.

His eyes dart around the bingo hall. A banner at the front announces *Most, biggest prizes in Outaouais Region!*

The Frontiersman isn't sure if *most* and *biggest* belong in the same sentence. He looks at the caller, who is concealed behind an antique bingo ball machine that hasn't been used in years. The caller sips from a bucket-size coffee cup and drawls "O-23" into the microphone.

The Frontiersman doesn't understand how bingo numbers are chosen if not by a mechanism that snatches a numbered ball from a swarm of balls hurtling around a bingo ball drum. Is the caller simply calling whatever number they choose? Is this not an invitation for malfeasance? *If you call O-27 next, I'll share the contents of my Spa Basket with you.*

"I-49 and O-27" The caller quickens his pace.

O-27? The Frontiersman stiffens. He looks at his cards but is unable to concentrate. What Os were called? 27, but what else? 32? I-forty-something? He is beset by doubt. What's to stop the Bingo caller from playing his own set of cards while calling the game and announcing whatever numbers they need to win?

The caller calls "N-42, G97, O-23, I-12."

The tension returns to the Frontiersman's shoulders. An ancient finger reaches into his field of vision and points at the N-42 square on one of his cards. It withdraws shakily.

"B-17, G-23, I-98, 0-12, N-14."

How is anyone supposed to remember all these numbers? Especially given the age of the players! The Frontiersman watches a wizened woman in a wheelchair who looks like she's two hundred years old struggle to lift her dabber. He grits his teeth. He won't be beaten by someone more senior than Canada itself. He begins to dab at his cards. If he's unsure a number has been called, he dabs anyway.

"B-45," the caller calls.

The Frontiersman's concentration is interrupted when a nearby player – late-sixties, immaculately coiffed, wearing either a knit sweater or a throw rug – claps her hands together. She carefully caps her dabber and opens her mouth to shout BINGO when the Frontiersman shouts BINGO!

"BINGO!" the caller echoes. "Let's have us a look at the winning card. Step right up!"

The Frontiersman shoots up from the table with both arms raised.

"Today we have two winners!" he announces, pointing at throw rug.

He strides towards the confused woman and hauls her to her feet.

"We did it!" he beams while grabbing her card.

"Which prize will you choose?" he asks her. "The dashboard wagging head dog or the embroidered plant hanger? You get dibs."

The bingo caller hears this.

"If you want to go home with junk, play elsewhere," he growls.

His indignation is seconded by the PA system, which fills the hall with feedback. Hearing aids are fiddled with.

"This is Outaouais' winningest bingo," the caller reminds the players. "Today's prize proves that beyond doubt!"

On cue, a bingo hall assistant yanks back the sheet covering what the Frontiersman thought was a post-Bingo buffet. And there, in as pristine condition as the day it rolled from the assembly line fifty years ago and was driven into a garage where it lived until being donated to Outaouais' winningest bingo, is a 1970 Buick Estate station wagon. Its two-tone paint job, vomit green on top, fake wood panelling below, shines like a hoard of oxidized Spanish treasure. Its roof rack is big enough to carry an entire second car. The assistant pops the hood and a blue whale, the largest mammal on earth, opens its jaws. The bingo hall's powerful neon lights barely manage to illuminate the Buick's massive four-fifty-five big-block V8. Three-gear automatic transmission, full vinyl interior, innumerable ashtrays. The purity of ingredients and humility of design speak for themselves.

The Frontiersman is so awestruck he nearly loses control of throw rug, who is trying to wriggle free. He recovers, tightens his grip on her arm and directs a smile into the face of the ferocious lap dog staring back at him.

"That embroidered plant hanger will look amazing above your folding TV tray dinner table," he assures the irate Pomeranian.

"Go to hell!" she hisses. "*Le Buick est à moi.*"

The untrained pet chewing its master's slipper. The Frontiersman imagines having to share the Buick with crocheted hallway runner. He sees her slipper-wearing feet alternating between gas and break, gas and break, as she strains to see over the dashboard, one that is rendered in the finest vinyl woodgrain finish. The final straw are the many dings, scrapes and gouges that deface both sides of the Buick. Cruel reminders that modern cities are no longer suitable grazing grounds for such a primordial beast.

The Frontiersman and his Sunday driver co-pilot are nearing the front of the hall when he sees a side door labelled basement. In a fluid gesture, he opens the door and shoves his prize co-claimant into the gloom that may contain a flight of stairs. In a last act of defiance, she grabs his beautiful curls and rips the wig from his head. He slams the door shut, muting her cries.

"Bathroom break," he informs the room.

He slaps her winning bingo card down in front of the caller. While the winning card is being checked, the assistant snaps his photo. Seconds later, the Frontiersman's bewildered expression framed by a computer-generated gilded frame is reproduced on the hall's many large television screens.

"We have a winner!" the caller announces.

A police cruiser creeps past the bingo. Its occupants compare their surroundings with the wanted image taped to the dashboard. The driver scans left, and the officer riding shotgun looks right and sees several enormous images of the fugitive.

He tells the driver to back up. The Frontiersman tells the bingo caller to hand him the key. The cop at the wheel reverses and comes to a halt in front of the bingo hall. The Frontiersman grabs the Buick's key and seconds later turns it in the ignition. The cops exit their cruiser. Their service weapons exit their holsters. A cloud of exhaust exits the Buick's tailpipe as the V8 roars to life. The Frontiersman reverses down the hall's central aisle until drawing abreast with his pack. He hauls it through the driver window. The cops enter the hall, guns drawn. Bingo patrons scatter like snails. One of the cops is opening and closing his mouth, but the whinnying and neighing of three hundred and fifty purebred stallions beneath the Buick's hood make it impossible for the Frontiersman to understand what is being said. A bullet pings off the Buick and ends the Frontiersman's lip-reading attempts. He jams the column shift into drive and stomps on the accelerator. The Minotaur emerges from its lair.

It's a shame that horses only neigh and whinny and don't roar or sound like howler monkeys. Because the sound the Buick makes as it rockets through the windowed facade of the bingo hall, brushing aside the cop cruiser as though it were a box full of donuts, is memorable. Even if most of the people who hear the sound are very old, deaf and likely to soon forget it. If no one was around to witness the Big Bang, did it still go bang? Yes, it did.

The Frontiersman massages the steering wheel of the careening Buick. It straightens out, and the land shark, a unique blend of colossal mammal and prehistoric predator, bottoms out as it sheers onto Boulevard Labrosse. A traffic light has the nerve to turn red, but the Frontiersman bends to nature's will and runs it. The Buick's solid steel bumper connects with a small, fuel-efficient family sedan that dared advance when the light turned green. A freight train hauling minerals, old-growth lumber and sausages made from Canadian beef meets an invasive fly species. The sedan is obliterated. Its multiple airbags save the occupants from instant death, although perhaps not from years of painful and expensive rehab.

Eighty-three seconds later, the Buick reaches its top speed of one hundred and twenty-four miles per hour. By the time it leaves behind shopping plazas and tinderbox subdivisions, it has become a streak. A flash. A smear of green and brown. Effortlessly, it adapts to its new environment of low, dark forests. Hundreds of the trillions of insects that call the surrounding underbrush home have already fallen victim to its windshield. The Frontiersman rests one hand lightly on the steering wheel. With the other, he turns the selector dial of the Buick's radio. An AM station is playing Willie Nelson's *On the road again*. The Frontiersman turns up the volume as he, the Buick and Willie rocket through Wilson's Corners. A right then left, then right, then left again evasive maneuver puts them on a horizontal surface that only someone from Missouri or Alaska would call a road. Skulking wildlife watches in awe as the proto-predator stampedes past. Several miles later, the Frontiersman is lost to the world.

Part II

The Ballet of Freedom — An Interlude

When possible, always know of multiple ways out of a mall,
office building, Tim Hortons – Survivalist Mantra

Happy Days

The following weeks are among the happiest In the Frontiersman's life, and he moves from one unoccupied hinterland cabin to the next. This happens mostly at night when people's inability to see in the dark forces them to use interior lights, which lets burglars or would-be squatters know if a place is occupied. Cottage owners trying to save on their electricity bill should not be surprised to find themselves face-to-face with an intruder as they feel their way to a late-night bathroom visit or midnight snack. Sometimes the arrival of a cottage's rightful owners catches the Frontiersman by surprise, and he is forced to clear out precipitously. A leap from a bedroom window. A hurried duck-like waddle from the outhouse into the underbrush. A hasty retreat in a borrowed canoe. Not paying rent is great, but it is not without its inconveniences. For starters, you have no right to be where you are, and you can't call the landlord when something breaks. But on the whole, the Frontiersman adapts to his new surroundings the way successful flora and fauna will acclimatize to evolving weather patterns. While some species wither and perish, others will flourish, sometimes even growing their roots through the empty eyeball sockets and into the cold but nutritious brain matter of their less flexible predecessors.

The Frontiersman might be behind on rent, but he is neither a quitter nor a complainer. What is there to be gained by capitulating and squatting dejectedly in some swamp just because the mosquitoes and black flies but also horse flies blot out the sun, humidity is at one hundred percent, and no fish has nibbled since dawn last week? Firstly, what are you doing fishing in a swamp, and secondly, you've just described a picture-perfect summer day in Canada, so get over yourself! Like a snake slithering from its skin, the Frontiersman discards his ego and instead embraces industrial-grade bug repellent, petty theft, and whatever opportunities fate deposits in his path.

The Buick, as prophesied, becomes the Frontiersman's retreat, larder, and armoury. A cape of skillfully glued-on branches and moss and landscape scenes rendered in permanent marker enhances the Buick's paint job and natural invisibility. Its interior soon becomes a cozy den of scavenged goods. Sleeping bags and cushions from front porch couches mingle with canned food, après-Soleil and mosquito coils. There's also a Mossberg shotgun, a rich and varied library of paperbacks, adult magazines, and several ounces of very presentable homegrown. Few of the corner stores the Frontiersman frequents when his stock of hard liquor and spam runs low have a more complete inventory.

The Frontiersman even begins to keep a diary. One without date or place.

One entry reads: *Was just sitting there looking at the moon reflect off the lake when a single falling pinecone wiggled the lake and shattered the moon. Now imagine the power of an entire forest.*

Another records *Am pretty sure the half-pound of mushrooms I ate were magic. The worst is over, but until the forest stops talking, me and the Mossberg are staying put.*

Unfortunately, the diary provides no clues as to where the Frontiersman *stayed put.* If anything, the diary clarifies that the Frontiersman's new habitat covered a vast territory. Another entry, titled *End of the road,* reads: *Who knew Ontario, Quebec and Nunavut share a border.* The fact they don't makes us wonder where the Frontiersman was when he made this observation. Had he made it to a place no one had been before? Were the mushrooms still in play? How much of the Buick's trunk and roof rack were dedicated to spare gas cans? As is always the case when someone goes off the grid, questions begin piling up.

Only with great effort does the Frontiersman finish reading the *Settler and his Wife.* His initial excitement, fueled by the sneak preview of graphic sexual content, soon yielded to dismay. As with many historical novels, the author's attempt to establish credibility resulted not in thrilling scenes of savagery and bloodshed but in the meticulous listing of era-specific minutiae. The first third of the novel was dedicated to the uneventful seventeenth-century lives of early Quebec *Habitants.* Dense chapters full of lace curtains, chaperoned dances and the teapot tempests that will fester in any boondock backwater. By the middle of the book, the habitant finally works up the courage to flee the societal doldrums of Lower Canada and becomes a backwoods trapper.

Deep in the forests of Gaspésie, the novel pulled a quick one on the Frontiersman. While toughing it out in the ever-deepening outback, the habitant discovers his penchant for men and engages in a Broke Back Mountain-style relationship with a young native. The Frontiersman wonders whether it's the sexual versatility of these hinterland lovebirds that has allowed them to escape the wrath of today's implacable post-colonial, queer theory inquisitors. The same ones who had first chastised and then censored Robinson Crusoe, the Frontiersman's childhood hero, until Robinson got tired of the harassment and willingly relocated from the required reading curriculum to the peace and quiet of the banned book list. The arrival of the settler's wife from France ends the habitant's brush with homo-eroticism.

That's right. Before immigrating to the New World and exploring the nature of New France but also his own sexual nature, the habitant had taken a wife as was the custom at the time.

The wife finds every aspect of Lower Canada pathetic and barbaric. After countless passages dedicated to the trapper's Catholic guilt that is both assuaged and worsened by hasty masturbation in his birch bark canoe, ones witnessed by forests "swept up in the cacophonic explosions of fall colouring," the Frontiersman welcomes the French wife's incessant bitching. A sentiment not shared by the habitant who begins taking "prolonged trips upriver." Finally, the wife catches the habitant and a native smoking each other's peace pipes. Fearing that news of his unnatural sexual behaviour will make it back to the capital, the settler moves deeper into the woods. The increasing distance from early Quebec's impersonation of civilization soon becomes proportional to the wife's unhappiness. Under increasing conjugal pressure, the settler stops frequenting his native lover and even manages to "perform his marital duties, if only perfunctorily." Seasons pass, and the wife doesn't get pregnant. One day she confronts him.

"If you'd fuck me more than once a year, I might get pregnant," she says with characteristic French directness.

She has a point. If you intend to get someone pregnant by having sex with them only once every twelve months, your timing had better be spot on. The wife is deafened by her biological clock and thoroughly fed up with shitty cabins overlooking dark lakes that couldn't look less like the Cote d'Azur if they tried.

"Or have you found yourself another Indian friend?" she grills the habitant in a terse scene that takes place in their wilted vegetable patch.

Although this is not an unreasonable line of inquiry, especially given the habitant's past behaviour and well-documented appetites, the wife's derisive tone and bad-cop, worse-cop gambit causes the trapper to lose it. Wordlessly, he storms to the water's edge and constructs a crude wooden cage out of branches and reeds. Then he returns to the vegetable patch and drags his wife to the cage by her hair. He crams her into the cage and rows wife, cage and canoe into the middle of the lake. Not even as the cage teeters on the edge of the canoe does the wife stop insulting her lame-duck husband. Her last words are, "You wouldn't dare. You don't have the balls." Turns out the habitant does. The Frontiersman wonders whether the bubbles that rise from the sinking cage to the lake's surface contain encapsulated insults.

Now free again, the habitant spends several seasons cruising native encampments. Sometimes he gets beaten up by men sporting ponytails and leather loincloths when he is caught spying on them as they bathe beneath waterfalls, but all in all, it is a happy time for him.

Maybe due to having grown as tired of *The Settler and his Wife* as the Frontiersman, the novel's author introduces a distant relative of the drowned wife. Introducing a brand new character in the last quarter of any book is sketchy at best, but sometimes an author's hands are tied. The Frontiersman briefly considers setting fire to the book but instead reads on and learns that the distant relative wields considerable influence in the budding colony. The relative also insists on an investigation into the wife's disappearance. There follows a plot twist that the Frontiersman deems cheap but is willing to forgive because it promises to bring the book to a quick end. The constables charged with investigating the wife's disappearance happen to show up when the trapper destroys a beaver dam on the lake where he sank his wife. As they are chatting on the remains of the dam and over the sound of the water rushing from the lake, the wife's cage and waterlogged remains come to light. The settler is apprehended, returned to the capital in chains and sentenced to hang. His last thought before the trap door beneath his feet clangs open is *Thank goodness my dirty little secret is safe.*

"Thank God this fucking book is finally finished," the Frontiersman says. A believer in the importance of literary discourse, the Frontiersman leaves the novel beside the hole and not in the pit of the outhouse. This gesture will allow future outhouse users to form their own opinions of the novel. Even if these opinions are limited to, *I'm in luck! I forgot to bring toilet paper and have just been saved by this wonderful book!* The Frontiersman is an open-minded reader. He will read Wilbur Smith as readily as he will Vince Flynn.

On va tout faire péter, câlisse!

Occasionally the Frontiersman watches the news or reads a local newspaper. Although the police double murder and country-wide manhunt have meandered from the first page to the journalistic no man's land behind the sports section, regular supposed sightings and the fact that a cop killer can expect no quarter are enough to keep the story alive. The Frontiersman is well aware of his status as public enemy, and when his migrations force him from gravel back roads onto asphalted thoroughfares, he travels at night and only uses the Buick's running lights. More than one deer has been obliterated by a speeding, two-and-a-half-ton moss-covered log with mood lighting. The carcass of a pulverized moose, an incident that crumpled the Buick's cast iron front fender mouldings, led to media speculations of a mega predator and an uptick in the sale of large calibre hunting rifles. On rare occasions, when the human need for kinship can no longer be ignored, the Frontiersman frequents out-of-the-way taverns. Here he plays pool, drinks whiskey, and if he's drunk enough and there's a jukebox, he even dances. Or at least stumbles drunkenly around the room, clinging to the backs of chairs, gun racks, or women's racks. Every patron of these frontier outposts has their own version of this steel-toe ballet solo. This traditional and interpretative dance of the inhabitants of *terra incognita*: this heart-wrenching cry for love or, failing that, at least a drunken make-out session. The footwork is never the same.

Frequenting these modern-day trading posts is not without risks. Fellow patrons are, without fail lonely, drunken individuals whose initial bonhomie can quickly sour. Women are exceedingly rare and have either barricaded themselves behind the bar, have already been claimed or are working. Which woman in her right mind would get into the back of a camouflaged 1970 Buick Estate after midnight with only one thing on the agenda? But there's a lid for every pot, and the Frontiersman's soft brown eyes, gentle demeanour and round after round of paid drinks that alter reality and lower the bar have resulted in several parking lot conquests.

The saying *A rolling stone gathers no moss* can be interpreted differently. In a literal reading, a giant boulder detaches from a mountain range and barrels downhill toward a cute and unsuspecting Alpine village. This boulder is unlikely to have lichen growing on it when it obliterates the village because even fast-growing lichen couldn't keep up with its precipitous descent. A more anthropomorphic interpretation implies that any human who chooses not to settle down is unlikely to become a big fish in a small pond. And while life on the road can be lonely, smelly and uncomfortable, adherents to nomadism don't spend their existence accumulating junk or getting caught up in petty local disputes. Which is precisely what happens when a flyer falls through the mail slot of a cabin the Frontiersman has been squatting for several weeks.

The flyer reads: *Save nature and make the world a better place!* A town hall meeting is scheduled for the following evening. The Frontiersman, enraged by the thought of big industry decimating his new-found habitat, decides to attend. When he pulls into the town hall's parking lot, he sees it's crammed with Toyota Prius' and Subarus. There's not a pickup truck in sight.

"Strange," he muses, overseeing the first signs of trouble.

"Donate to the cause?" a girl at the front door asks. "Buy a badge?"

The girl is cute, and the Frontiersman says he'll buy two. He hands her a five-dollar bill. She tells him that each badge costs fifteen dollars. Instead of laughing in her face, the Frontiersman hands over the equivalent of a quarter tank of gas for the Buick. Ever since he ditched the Amex Centurion, he's been on a tight budget.

"Thirty bucks for two stupid friggin badges!" he thinks, backing away and bumping into a snack table.

Instead of finding Nanaimo bars or hash brownies, the Frontiersman is confronted with gluten-free muffins and fair-trade apple cider and recoils in disgust. The meeting begins, and the Frontiersman takes position at the back of the hall.

"I'll get straight to business," the speaker says. "Most of us here tonight own a second home or a sizeable lakeside property. Some for as long as five years already."

"Five years and three months!" someone interrupts.

The speaker nods to acknowledge this exceptional land tenure and continues.

"That makes us part of the local community."

92

Applause. The Frontiersman notices that many attendees display expressions in which concern and condescension are flatmates. Or roommates. Bedmates?

"And yet," the speaker says indignantly and hotly, "long-term residents regularly exclude us from local decision-making."

"That's because the locals are poor Francophones who hate us because we're rich Anglos with fat government pensions," someone in the crowd reflects with surprising acuity and unwelcome frankness.

"Someone took a shit on the windshield of my Prius when I was in town last week," someone else says.

The speaker fears being brought off track by an avalanche of petty grievances and talks over the crowd.

"As members of this community but also as former members of parliament and the senate, we'll pull strings and ensure that the following legislation gets passed."

"My second cousin once dated the prime minister," someone seeking to improve their social standing shouts.

The speaker holds up a finger.

"An immediate end to all forest harvesting in a radius of one hundred, no, one thousand kilometres. Exceptions will be granted for the creation of bike paths or scenic lookouts."

A second finger pops from his palm.

"A moratorium on all new construction."

The speaker pauses to address Larry, a senior partner at the speaker's law firm who looks worried. "Don't worry, Larry. The permit for your new boathouse, guesthouse, spa buildings and four-storey cottage extension will be approved."

Larry, relieved, nods. Finger number three appears.

"That the local Walmart be forced to stock organic produce."

The speaker pauses to catch his breath. It's a mistake. Demands fill the hall.

"No more pesticides!"

"No more motorboats on lakes. Only canoes."

"And no more backwater hicks driving ATVs."

"No more hunting! Hunting is murder!"

The Frontiersman has heard enough and slips from the hall. He walks to the edge of the parking lot and lights a cigarette. An energetic, out-of-tune rendition of *Bella Ciao* drifts from the town hall's windows. The smell of gasoline drifts from two twenty-litre gas cans being unscrewed nearby. The Frontiersman retreats from view as two figures advance on the town hall. It's clear from their movements that they're no strangers to gas cans. The two individuals about to set fire to a town hall full of retired ministers, senators, federal judges, and the who-was-who of Canadian industry have spent their entire lives handling Jerry cans. Filling ATVs with awkwardly located gas tanks, topping up snowmobiles with frozen fuel caps or servicing chainsaws requiring a blend of different additives. As for setting things alight, piles of garbage, the recently insured barn that was a teardown, the ex-girlfriend's new boyfriend's trailer; you name it, they've torched it.

Having expertly encircled the town hall with gasoline, the arsonists dribble a trail of gas into the parking lot.

"No more fuckers from Ottawa telling us how to live our lives, heh?" one of them says, then stoops and flicks his lighter.

The town hall is instantly engulfed in flames. The singing of *We are the world, we are the children* yields to cries of terror. There's violent pounding on the town hall's door, but it doesn't budge. Did the arsonists jam a wedge under the door, a simple but effective technique used by people whose lives are spent jimmy-rigging junk with nothing but binder twine and chicken wire? The Frontiersman despises know-it-all government assholes who view the world beyond their cubicle through the needle hole of policy as much as the next decent human being. Still, standing by as hundreds of people are burned alive somehow doesn't feel right.

The Frontiersman races to the Buick, guns the engine, and slams it into reverse. The Buick's tires throw up gravel as it speeds backwards across the wide expanse of parking lot. His plan is vague. If formalized, it would read something like *Breach wall, create escape hole.*

"Damn is it stuffy in here," the Frontiersman says.

It's true. Given its contents, it doesn't take much for the Buick to develop a strong, musty odour. The Frontiersman pushes a button on the dash, and the Buick's nearly two-meter-wide rear window glides down on its tracks. Instantly, the interior is flooded by a pleasant breeze. The breeze flows under the all-purpose mattress in the back of the Buick and pushes it against the roof. In the split second it takes the Frontiersman to shift his gaze from the momentarily obstructed rear view to the side view mirror, the town hall's thousand-gallon propane tank slips in and back out of view. Afraid he won't have enough momentum to punch a hole in the town hall wall, the Frontiersman floors the accelerator. The speeding Buick collides with the propane tank. The tank sheers from its footings as though it were a marble in Newton's cradle, accelerating from zero to top speed in the blink of an eye. Confused by the fact he's nowhere near the town hall and the sound of metal on Detroit steel, the Frontiersman looks in the rear view mirror and sees someone who is on fire stagger through a hole in the burning town hall.

"Mission accomplished," he concludes, enjoying the satisfaction of a job well done. He even pushes aside thoughts of his dented rear bumper. He slams the Buick into drive and peels out of the parking lot. By the time he passes the city limits sign, the Buick is well above the speed limit. So far, in fact, that a traffic camera snaps a photo of the Buick and its driver.

Inside the town hall, the propane tank has upended the conscionable snack table and lies engulfed in flames.

"Ban propane!" someone shouts. "We'll use solar instead!"

The propane tank handles the criticism poorly and explodes. Because it is a new-generation tank permanently connected by pipeline to Quebec's province-wide propane infrastructure, it is full to the brim. The gigantic explosion rips apart the town hall and the political activism that was brewing within it. The ensuing shock waves expand in concentric circles, like those caused by the falling pine cone and recorded in the Frontiersman's diary. But instead of gently lapping at the lily pads at the edge of the lake and maybe causing a frog to lose its balance or a turtle to get a face full of lake water, these shock waves flatten the town hall's town and ignite the surrounding forests. Vinyl siding, packages of pancake mix, loaves of white bread, chainsaw oil and bags of discount dog food, but also the people whose lives were characterized by these modern conveniences are incinerated or hurled into the air. Or both. In one case, someone miraculously survives the huge fireball and being hurled through the air but ultimately succumbs to smoke inhalation when their getaway is hampered by a twisted ankle.

The explosion fills the Buick's rearview mirror with a flash of light, and the Frontiersman eases off the gas. Which is why he is just under the speed limit as he passes a lurking highway patrol car. Not for the first time, the officer in the patrol car ponders the existence of a sixth sense that permits motorists to detect the presence of lurking patrol cars. The officer's musings are cut short by an emergency call about a town hall burning out of control. The officer races to the scene of the explosion, his cruiser skidding to a halt before a backdrop of utter devastation. Why police officers insist on driving so aggressively is anyone's guess. Who else crushes the accelerator each time they buy donuts or meet an equally bored colleague in a deserted parking lot for a chat? Why screech to a halt each time you have to park? Why not just feather the brakes before rolling to a stop? Is it because cops don't pay for their own gas or the brake pads of their cruisers that need weekly replacing?

Be this as it may, the cruiser's skidding tires flick a brightly glowing ember, which is all that is left of the town hall. The flicked ember bounces across the parking lot and, after teetering on the edge of the shorn-off propane pipeline, falls in. A hole in one. The ember gathers speed as it plummets ever deeper into the pipeline, which gains in girth as it descends into the earth. Like an asteroid fighting its way through the earth's atmosphere, the ember's edges glow not only red but hot white. By the time it plunks into the pipeline's capacious main line, it has reached a temperature of nearly five-hundred degrees Celsius. Which is, unfortunately, precisely the temperature required for propane to self-ignite. In a game of broken telephone, trillions of francophone propane molecules pass the word through Quebec's network of underground pipelines.

It's time to blow.

Hein?

On va tout faire péter, câlisse!

Despite what many people think, Quebec's doomed pipelines are not simple metal tubes through which gas is pumped with the help of repurposed ceiling fans. They are state-of-the-art and have pump and choke stations, phase separators, condensers, dehydration and sulphur recovery systems and anti-blowback valves. They were, however, designed by anglophone engineers who failed to take the vehemence of francophone social movements into account. Most cultural differences can be glossed over, this one's the exception. A propane molecule named Jacques is the first to combust. Then Françoise and Jean-Pierre follow suit. Then the twenty siblings of the Tremblay molecular family join the fun. Soon *le parté* is in full swing.

Meanwhile, the Frontiersman is squinting, driving with one hand and digging through the crap in the central console in search of his sunglasses. Such is the glare of the fiery glow that has engulfed the horizon. Sometimes he even drives with his eyes shut. The Frontiersman has never seen anything like it. Is it a rare firefly mating ritual? A large city he's never heard of? A cosmic sign? The Frontiersman isn't one to discard esoteric theories out of hand, and as he's already driving towards the horizon, decides to follow what might be an astral divination. He also turns on the radio, and the Buick's speakers crackle to life. Especially the bass speaker, which erupts with a thud of bass so loud it lifts the Buick's rear end into the air. Why has he never heard this song before? Did the bass player's instrument have only a single massive string?

The Buick's rear end returns to earth with a crash and shower of sparks. Which can't be said for the province's recently expanded propane storage facility in Valleyfield, where six hundred thousand gallons of highly pressurized propane just blew up. The resulting explosion wipes Valleyfield from the face of the map and the earth.

Fugitive Sasquatch

Social media, faster than human conscience, more compelling than our basest instinct and as unfiltered as the murkiest micro-brew, is the first to carry news of the Valleyfield tragedy. At first, Montrealers react with a hefty dose of big-city cynicism. *Valleyfield*?! an oft-shared tweet begins. *Some crap suburb with half a canal that calls itself the Venice of Quebec? Who cares?* A meme of a smouldering crap suburb with half a canal entertains social media users for several minutes. #Valleyfield? Jemesouvienspas becomes the *de rigueur* tagline. A crowd-funding site dedicated to rebuilding an Instagram-friendlier version of Valleyfield raises twenty-five thousand dollars. A Montreal bartender becomes a sensation by inventing the *Valleyfield Flambé,* which causes throngs of rubber-necking hipsters to be treated for facial burns. Only hours later, with the now sober and disfigured party-goes still seated in the hard-plastic chairs of hospital waiting rooms, does the extent of the devastation and tragedy begin to emerge.

The Energir pipeline supplying the cities of Mirabel, Lachute and Mont-Tremblant, an overbuilt ski resort with Alpine architecture that fools no one, is no more. Camera footage taken from helicopters shows a flaming chasm where the pipeline once lay buried. Now a fiery ditch gouges its way through the landscape, with cities, suburbs, shopping plazas and small parcels of remaining nature burning out of control along its banks. Ditto for the TQM pipeline servicing southeastern Quebec, where the cities of Joliette, Pointe-du-Lac, Trois-Rivieres and Sherbrooke have been reduced to ash.

Dazed and burned, survivors stagger through the wreckage. Some are hauled away by badly singed wild animals, others die of other causes. The once-vibrant city of Montreal has somehow been spared but is subdued and kept alight only by scented candles. Quebec City, with its unique cultural heritage, European streetscape but also massive natural gas liquifying facility, is hardest hit. Despite attempts by the authorities to censor images, social media is soon awash with selfies of its melted downtown core and logjams of cadavers damming the St. Lawrence River.

Miraculously, the TransCanada pipeline has remained unscathed. The inhabitants of Ontario, of Canada's central provinces and people living as far as British Columbia and Whitehorse mourn Quebec's tragedy in emotional gatherings that feature poolside barbecues, hot showers, air conditioning and mixed drinks with lots and lots of crushed ice. The amount of ice is truly copious. A perspicacious news commentator wonders whether the tragedy has thrust Quebec back into the Dark Ages, a place from which it had only recently emerged.

And where is the Frontiersman during this period of terrible destruction, mass extinction and geopolitical upheaval? The Frontiersman is in the Buick with his eyes on the horizon. Although it's a strains on his eyes and he still hasn't found his sunglasses, he never loses it from view. Not even when the smoke from the explosions and fires reduce him to doing twenty miles an hour with the high beams on. Steadfastly, unerringly, he aims the Buick at it. Patiently too, because it never seems to get any closer. Is this because the intense glow now filling the Buick's vast windshield makes the horizon appear larger and further away? Or is it because when you reach one horizon, the one that was hiding behind it is already waiting? When the Frontiersman tires of pondering such questions, he honks the horn festively to accompany the largest and longest-lasting firework display he has ever witnessed. The Frontiersman can't say why, but he swears there's a sense of renewal in the air.

Inspired, he looks around for a car wash but can't see one. Instead, he pulls onto the shoulder and frees the Buick of its woodland camouflage. A mildewed pillow, his pillow, is sacrificed to revive the Buick's ample chrome. While applying elbow grease to the left front hubcap, he accidentally catches a whiff of his armpit. Later, when he regains consciousness, a glance in the now shiny hubcap confirms his worst fears. His time off-grid has reduced him to a near-animal state. He could pass for a hipster with his long beard and lumberjack appeal from a distance, but this distance would have to be half a mile or more. Anyone closer would see a wild-eyed fugitive. Rancid, threadbare, desperate.

Fortunately, the Frontiersman doesn't feel desperate. On the contrary, his decision to leave the bush has invigorated him, and he decides it's time for a roadside coffee and maybe a honey cruller. The Frontiersman's favourite thing about Quebec is that you can't drive more than five minutes without passing a *Dépanneur,* and four and a half minutes later, he parks and walks into Roland's Convenience. Fifteen seconds later, he is back in the Buick and laying serious rubber down highway fifty. A half minute later, a police officer answers the phone at the police station in the nearby town of Thurso.

"Thurso police," says the police officer.

"Guy," says Roland from Roland's Convenience. "It's me, Roland. That guy you're looking for? The guy who blew up the province? He just left my store. Eastbound on the fifty. Driving my grandmother's station wagon."

Thurso's police officer upends preconceived notions of bumbling rural cops by sprinting to his high-powered Dodge Charger police cruiser. His clean-shaven chin, no-nonsense haircut and ten-to-two hands on the wheel hint loudly at a worldview in which order and cleanliness figure prominently. There is no room in this universe, not even in the bleachers, for anyone who has willfully immolated half the province. News that his beloved Tante Pascale had been vaporized in her trailer park in Repentigny had snuffed out what little Christian forgiveness might once have lurked in the officer's soul.

He has just screeched to a halt at the top of the highway on-ramp when he hears the unmistakable farting purr of a V8's leaky head gasket. The four-fifty-five's Achilles heel. Imagine opening a fifty-year-old jar of jam. Of hot chilli pepper jam. There's no way that rubber seal is still gonna be nice and rubbery. Seconds later, the Buick flashes past, and a cruel grin befalls the officer's lips. He guns it and falls in behind the station wagon.

The Frontiersman is still smarting from the name-calling and unsubstantiated accusations made by the national press on display at Roland's Convenience when a police car appears in his rearview mirror. He glances at the speedometer, sees he's a smidgen and a half over the speed limit and eases off the accelerator. Using his fingers, he combs his hair. The cruiser doesn't budge. What the hell can the cop want? Then he remembers his photo on every front page, the one that was obviously taken by a traffic camera, and knows that they know. Or rather that they think they know. The headlines had not exercised constraint.

Murderous arsonist blows up Quebec.
La Belle Province destroyed by fugitive Sasquatch.
Quebec fait boom.

The Frontiersman doesn't understand. How could he have blown up Quebec? He doesn't even own a gas barbecue.

The Dodge Charger emits that aggressive electronic burp that cop cars make when they want something.

"Pull over," the burp says.

The Frontiersman eyes the shoulder. It's pathetically narrow. Nowhere near wide enough to adequately accommodate the Buick's girth. The officer thinks of his Tante Pascale's delicious mac and cheese casseroles, floors the Charger and rams the Buick. The cruiser's bullbar crumples.

"Like kicking a goddamn elephant," the officer mutters, tightening his grip on the steering wheel.

The Frontiersman is torn. Should he pull over and risk scratching the Buick and several life sentences? Does Quebec still have the death penalty? Will the province he is accused of blowing up give him a fair trial? Will his beloved Buick still be in the prison parking lot when he is released, likely decades from now? Do maximum security prisons even have long-term parking, and is it affordable?

The Frontiersman and the police cruiser pass a sign indicating the Grenville exit. The Frontiersman knows that Grenville and Hawkesbury are connected by a bridge and that Hawkesbury is in Ontario. This seals it. The Frontiersman knows he has to make it to Ontario. Only there does he stand a chance.

He yanks on the steering wheel and sheers across lanes of traffic. The Charger follows. At the bottom of the off-ramp, the Frontiersman turns right at a light without even pretending to slow. He knows he's racking up misdemeanours and flinches. Failure to indicate a lane change, not coming to a complete stop before turning right on red, arson, and mass murder on a province-wide scale. The Charger rams the Buick a second time, this time on an angle. The Buick fishtails dangerously.

"Ha!" the officer shouts, triumph in his voice.

"Fuck!" the Frontiersman shouts.

Then the Charger and its mangled bumper fall back.

"Ha!" the Frontiersman shouts prematurely.

Thurso's police officer floors the Charger, preparing to ram the Buick again. It races forward, but the Frontiersman sees it coming this time and stomps on the brakes. Two and a half tons of Buick Estate plus another half-ton of random stuff rolling around in the back lurch forward, and the Buick's rear end rises. Just enough for the hood of the inbound Charger to slip beneath it. When the Buick settles, the Charger feels and drives like an elephant is sitting on its chest. The Thurso police officer and Frontiersman are now like two circus clowns inside a two-person horse. Or elephant, but costumes with trunks and tusks are hard to sew and therefore more rare. The Frontiersman steers, the officer wags the tail. Despite their very different agendas, circumstances are forcing them to work together.

Cooperation goes very badly. After failing to push the Buick off the road, the officer changes tack, shifts into reverse and begins dragging the Frontiersman deeper into Quebec.

"No!" The Frontiersman shouts. "Anywhere but Quebec!"

He guns the Buick, but its rear wheels are off the ground and spin with no effect. A distant onlooker could easily mistake what is going on for two beetles, an angry black and white one and a non-consenting brown and green one, having sex. Finally, the elephantine Buick's weight pushes the Charger's undercarriage into the asphalt, and everything grinds to a halt. The Charger burps again.

"Get out of your vehicle. You are surrounded."

The Frontiersman looks around but sees no one. A handful of grain silos and the outline of Grenville straight ahead. And wheat fields. That's it. He wonders what makes cops tell such blatant lies and tries to judge the distance to the river. Can he sprint there before the cop shoots him in the back? He eyes the surrounding wheat fields and wishes they were harvest-ready corn fields capable of concealing professional basketball players. He imagines speedcrawling through the wheat, occasionally stopping to raise his head for orientation, a gopher inviting a trigger-happy hunter to target practice. He discards the idea.

Meanwhile, one and a half car lengths away, Thurso's police officer is coming to terms with the fact that he won't be able to apprehend the fugitive on his own. Reinforcements will have to be called. The lone wolf bounty hunter must share the reward and the glory.

"*Esti de callisse de callisse d'esti de callisse!*" the officer swears and pummels the Charger's dashboard with his fists.

His anger ripples along the rubber cover that protects the dashboard from UV rays and descends the vertical struts that attach the cruiser's body to the chassis. It loses none of its bloody intentions as it travels along the frame rails and into the radiator. When it reaches the cruiser's mauled hood, the officer's desire to kick his aunt's killer to within an inch of his life sends tiny but choppy waves through the sheet metal. One such wave dislodges the Buick, which slips off the Charger's hood and lands on the road with a crunch. Suddenly freed of its pachyderm and still in reverse, the police cruiser flies backwards down highway three forty-four. The Buick and the Frontiersman rocket through Grenville and engage the Long-Sault inter-provincial bridge at four times the recommended speed.

Up the Red River

What the Frontiersman needs is a plan. Or an outline of a plan. He settles for a motto. *Disappear* is his motto *for as long as necessary*. From the bridge, he sees a marina a short way downriver and guns the Buick. A small gun. Maybe even a bow and arrow and not a compound bow. Suddenly the Buick feels sluggish. Has it run out of gas? The gas gauge reads half full. Or does it know it's about to be abandoned? Is the sudden loss of power, the fact that it appears to be firing on only four or five of its mighty cylinders, its way of prolonging time with the Frontiersman? The Frontiersman feels tears well up in the Buick's headlights. His own eyes mist over. He knows there'll be no time for proper goodbyes. He skids into the marina parking lot and affectionately flicks the lid of the nearest ashtray.

"I'm gonna miss you," he croaks.

The Buick remains silent, but the Frontiersman knows how to interpret the silence, and it nearly breaks his heart. He hears distant sirens and stuffs some things into a sleeping bag. There's no time to be picky. Whatever fits. And some things that don't fit. But nothing else. He exits the Buick and does his best to look normal. Like a well-heeled pleasure craft owner out for a stroll. But the role doesn't come easily, so he changes roles and tries to look like a sailor with a sleeping bag gunny sack seeking employment on a tramp steamer. Only there are no tram steamers moored in the marina. Finally, the Frontiersman decides to be himself. Calmly, he takes stock of the boats moored to various piers. The marina is full of all kinds of boats. Motorboats mostly, but also sailboats and some boats that have been pulled out of the water and shrink-wrapped. What kind of captain would choose saran wrap over an iconic yellow mackintosh? He imagines racing away from pursuing police crafts on a windless day and discards anything with a sail. He can't explain why, but somehow he knows that motorboats aren't right either. Don't you have to fill them up every half hour? Aren't the heads cramped and maintenance costs prohibitive? Not to mention you're constantly passing someone who has a bigger one?

There! Leaning against the marina dumpster is an abandoned canoe. His patience and discernment have been rewarded. At first glance, it appears full of garbage, but upon closer inspection, he sees it's only half full. Two-thirds tops. The Frontiersman tips out the trash and throws in his sleeping bag. Afraid the fanatical cop might have followed him into Ontario, he eyes the bridge. At the far end, he sees the battered Charger and the officer standing at the open door, speaking into his radio.

Next, the Frontiersman tries to gauge whether the sirens have grown closer. He tries to remember how loud they were a few minutes ago but can't. He wonders if police have developed software that lowers the volume of sirens when they near a crime scene. This would allow them to sneak up on criminals who'd been lulled into complacency by a false sense of having gotten away with whatever crime they'd committed. He reminds himself not to rest on his laurels.

His stomach growls, reminding him he is ravenous. He eyes the convenience store across from the marina. Would spending the rest of one's life on the lam without proper supplies be foolish?

"Idiotic even," the Frontiersman mutters. "Possibly life-threatening."

He enters the convenience store, grabs a shopping cart and vanishes into the back, where he power shops. One cardboard box of canned spam. Twelve rolls of toilet paper. Two armfuls of assorted chocolate bars. Every can of sardines on the shelf. Mosquito repellent. To his surprise, he sees a blend of sunscreen and mosquito repellent and replaces the traditional bug spray with this new product.

"Evolve or perish," he thinks.

Then he thinks *candles* and adds a box to the shopping cart.

Ideally, the candles would be slow-burn, non-paraffin ones, but the Frontiersman is in a rush and hopes that wildlife isn't attracted to his box of vanilla, sage and coconut-scented ones. He adds salted crackers and a bottle of whiskey to the cart. And a bottle of gin and a second bottle of whiskey. And two large bottles of Canada Dry as mix, and some wrinkly limes, and four blocks of cheddar cheese, and a thirty-six pack of hotdogs. And waterproof matches.

The convenience store clerk asks the Frontiersman if he knows there's a regular supermarket up the road. The Frontiersman tells the clerk he likes to support local businesses. The clerk says the same guy owns the supermarket and convenience store. The Frontiersman tells the clerk that this is a robbery and to come out from behind the counter. The clerk does as he's told and gets locked in the bathroom. Before leaving, the Frontiersman fills a plastic bag with overpriced but appealing doohickeys on display near the check-out counter. This is how he comes to own a set of glow-in-the-dark fishing lures and a compass slash AM/FM radio.

Then he pushes the shopping cart back to the canoe, which is unnecessarily tricky because all four wheels swivel. Telling himself there'll be time to repack later, he dumps the cart's contents into the canoe, then nearly herniates his back dragging it to the put-in. After a final teary glance at the Buick, he shoves off. By the time the police sniffer dogs are clawing at the convenience store's bathroom door, the Frontiersman is long gone.

Or at least not visible from shore. Once out of the marina, the Frontiersman paddles his way upstream toward the Red River. Why he does this isn't immediately clear. Is he looking for an additional upper-body workout? Does he want to catch a final final glimpse of his beloved Buick, on which some river bird has already shat? Or is it because the Red River is the only nearby river that stretches inland where it loses itself in an acned and impenetrable wilderness. No fugitive in their right mind would choose to lay low on the Ottawa River. Claimed and tamed long ago by industrial farming and recently recolonized and asphalted to within an inch of its banks by retirement communities, the Ottawa River may as well be a parking lot. Or a highway. Or the main artery of a shopping mall. And although going up the Red River means going back into Quebec, not all decisions have the luxury of being made in the quiet of a reading room with a well-stocked bar trolley. The Frontiersman is low on time and options.

Hawkesbury and the marina are also swarming with police, and the Frontiersman has to keep out of sight. He does this by paddling quietly and hunching over. When police boats pass, he hides under pontoon docks on which families are arguing and getting drunk. Or getting drunk and then arguing. The Frontiersman is also not above clinging to slow-moving and unsuspecting houseboats. To camouflage the canoe, he cuts his sleeping bag into strips and drapes the brown and stained material over the gunwale. He also removes his recent convenience store acquisitions from their bright and crinkly plastic wrappers that could easily reflect the sun and catch the eye or ear of a police sniper. Soon there is a hotdog, sardine and salted cracker bouillabaisse sloshing in the bottom of the canoe. He nibbles at a soggy cracker and wonders whether removing everything from its packaging was perhaps premature.

His upriver progress is painfully slow, and dusk finds him pulling the canoe into the reeds and underbrush at the mouth of the Red River. Blisters cover his hands. He gulps greedily from the bottle of gin and passes out. For the next twelve hours, he is the primary source of nourishment for tens of thousands of ravenous mosquitoes.

The Frontiersman is awoken by a mosquito building a nest for its young in his nose. He snorts and destroys the insect's dream of home ownership and leaving an inheritance to its offspring. Hundreds of mosquito bites have swollen his eyes nearly shut. If he had a mirror, which he doesn't, he'd see that his entire face is swollen half shut. Undeterred, he wolfs down a hearty breakfast of cold cheddar hotdogs and whiskey. Referring to the public library's copy of *The Great Traverse*, which somehow is still with him, he charts the next leg of his journey.

The Red River, he reads, *dumps into the Ottawa River after a series of rapids. Bathing downriver from the Kilmar paper mill is only recommended if you're not overly punctilious about skincare or are already afflicted by skin pigmentation issues.*

The Frontiersman shuts the book. He also shuts his nose to block out the smell of freshly brewed coffee wafting from a nearby campsite. He squashes a mosquito that has returned for more of his blood, pushes the canoe into the water and hops in. The bottom of the canoe crunches against rocks, and the Frontiersman clambers out and begins hauling the canoe upstream. The occupants of the enormous recreational vehicles lining the riverfront wave at him. The Frontiersman waves back.

"You're going the wrong way," the campground joker shouts.

But not every man's freedom lies in the same direction, and the Frontiersman continues pulling his canoe through the shallow but fast-moving water. As the current grows stronger, footing becomes a problem. He slips once, nearly rolls his ankle but recovers. Then he slips again, and this time goes down hard. Only a rib-jarring dive keeps the canoe from disappearing downriver. One that tips the canoe. Holding onto the canoe with one hand, the Frontiersman wrests what he can of his supplies from the greedy current with the other. Breathing is agonizing, and he wonders if he's broken ribs. Brightly-coloured inflatable rafts carrying tourists float past downstream. He receives numerous thumbs-ups but turns his face away from the cameras. Four hours and a hundred feet later, he drags the canoe into the shrubs of a sandbank and inventories his belongings.

One block of cheddar cheese, two boxes of water-logged waterproof matches, one bottle of whiskey, some salty crackers, the *Great Traverse*. He carefully wraps everything in the single remaining strip of sleeping bag and crams this improvised dry bag under the canoe's front seat. Here he's delighted to find three hotdogs, which he washes down with a few nips at the whiskey bottle. Then he lays himself spread-eagle in the sun to dry and read.

Portaging, he reads. *Without a doubt portaging is the worst thing you'll do in your entire life. Unless you marry a woman from Puerto Rico.*

The Frontiersman wonders why authors insist on littering their writing with experiences garnered from their personal lives. He pictures himself carrying his canoe across a beautiful Puerto Rican beach. Tanned and curvaceous locals—the Frontiersman hopes one of them will ask for his hand in marriage—beckon him to enter a tent where he knows a sensual massage awaits. How bad can portaging be? A horse fly not much smaller than a horse nose dives him.

He reads on. *If you can't get someone else to do it for you, your best approach is to suss out your portage route before you set off into the woods with a sixteen-foot canoe on your head.*

"We'll see about that," the Frontiersman snorts. He doesn't appreciate being lectured.

Did early Polynesian explorers paddle their flimsy outrigger canoes halfway to the horizon for a recce before confronting the vastness of the Pacific? The Frontiersman thinks not. To hell with whoever wrote *The Traverse*. The Frontiersman reminds himself not to judge a book by the author's photograph. Instead, he transforms the improvised dry bag into an impromptu fanny pack and wrestles the canoe above his head. The canoe weighs seventy pounds, and after an awkward tap dance in the shallows on slimy rocks, he keels over backwards and lands painfully on and in the canoe.

"Nice one!" a kayaker calls who glides past in an inflatable twenty-five-pound Intex Challenger.

The Frontiersman checks to see if he's broken his back. He doesn't think so. Somehow he manages to tow his canoe from the sandbank to the river's left bank. Here he re-attempts the portage position and manages a few staggering steps before getting snarled in the plastic rings that once held together a six-pack. He goes down hard again, this time ending up under the canoe. He decides to rest and, being of a forgiving nature, pulls the *Great Traverse* from his fanny pack.

In ancient cultures, he reads, *there was less leisure time than in today's world. Egyptians, Ottomans, Greeks and Vikings would have considered carrying a canoe through a hostile environment less a sign of middle-class leisure than an idiotic waste of time. That is why they employed vast numbers of slaves to move their ships for them. Warships or early cargo ships, not fragile and pointless one or two-person paddle-driven crafts that require ongoing maintenance and take up half the basement when stored. Early ships were pulled over a bed of logs by slaves toiling at the end of hemp ropes. When a log had travelled from the front to the back of the ship, it was carried back to the front by sandal-wearing forced labour. And so it went, until either a hemp rope snapped and the ship was sent hurtling backwards down some cliff or had reached its destination.*

The Frontiersman enjoys a soggy cracker, cheddar cheese and whiskey snack and considers this new information. The outline of a hint of a hunch begins to crystallize. A prolonged afternoon nap also happens, and when the Frontiersman awakes, parched but rested, it is dark. He hides the canoe in a brambly thicket and walks the two hours back into Grenville, where he sticks to back alleys and shadows. A dart-in, dart-back-out mission involving the Tim Horton dumpster is rewarded with a lap full of half-eaten breakfast sandwiches and week-old muffins. The Frontiersman was raised not to leave as much as a scrap on his plate and doesn't start now. Later, he stops at a dripping fire hydrant and drinks his fill. On his third round of town, he hits the jackpot. A canoe-carrying dolly is poking out of an unlocked shed. The Frontiersman had been ready to improvise. Stolen bicycle wheels, duct tape, snow shovel handle. Fearing he might anger the gods, he didn't dare dream of a purpose-built canoe dolly. Over the fence and in and back out of the unlocked shed he goes. Two hours later, he's back at his canoe.

In what little is left of that same night, the Frontiersman and his canoe reach the town of Kilmar. A feat made possible by the canoe dolly and Tim Horton sugar high. Dawn finds the Frontiersman reading an information panel on the outskirts of Kilmar. *Initially settled by loggers that supplied the town's paper mill with cellulose, Kilmar reached a peak population of 502 in 1967 when the town's asbestos mine ushered in a Gold Rush atmosphere. Between the closing of the asbestos mine in 2011 and text messaging's sustained attack on longhand letter writing, Kilmar is currently going through a rough patch.*

"Like me," the Frontiersman empathizes, letting his gaze wander.

Someone, maybe Cindy, has scrawled *for a good time call Cindy* next to a crudely drawn vagina and a telephone number. The Frontiersman eagerly pats down his pockets but realizes he doesn't have a phone. The Kilmar paper mill makes its presence known with a waft of rotten eggs. The Frontiersman thinks that camping upwind from the mill would be preferable and studies the surrounding trees to see which way the wind is blowing. The crowns of a nearby stand of poplars bend this way and that. Sometimes they seem to go in circles. The Frontiersman takes that as an invitation to camp anywhere and retreats to the edge of the litter-strewn picnic area. Where vandalized picnic tables and used condoms meet the forest, he discovers blueberries which he stuffs into his mouth. He wrestles the canoe and dolly into the thick underbrush and gets badly scratched. Then he realizes that the underbrush is poison ivy. Overcome by exhaustion, he falls deeply asleep on a wonderfully soft and springy termite mound.

By the time the Frontiersman awakens, the termites have burrowed deep into his facial cavities. The sensation of having hundreds of uninvited beings not only trespass on your personal space but also be industrious in your sinuses and in that thin layer of fat between the skin of your face and your skull is highly unnerving. But once again, the Frontiersman refutes panic and stays calm. Using the whiskey bottle as a neti pot, he rinses his face with the remains of the blended whiskey in which malt plays second fiddle to grain. Anyone who boasts about drinking a stiff Bloody Mary after a long night out is unlikely to have experienced the searing, sobering pain of neti potting the inside of your face with hooch. As the termites vacate their subcutaneous digs, streaming from ears and nostrils, the Frontiersman suffers a revelation.

Revelations must exist in varying sizes and degrees, like pizzas or earthquakes. And although we will never know the exact amplitude or choice of toppings of the one that befell the Frontiersman in Kilmar's less-than-welcoming picnic area, there can be no doubt that its effect was profound. The Frontiersman's eyes, although bloodshot and swollen, are suddenly aglow with the crazed look of the religious zealot. Their slight yellowness speak no longer of a diet of cheddar hotdogs and grain spirits but of a higher purpose. The Frontiersman crunches on a mouthful of termites that had foolishly chosen his esophagus as their escape route, turns on his heel, and, leaving canoe, canoe dolly and even the sleeping bag fanny pack behind, strides into the underbrush. Thorn-studded branches, festering second growth, uneven rock-strewn ground, and the absence of sun-dappled clearings and babbling brooks, close behind him like a curtain. Instead of an ovation, there is the buzzing of insects. The clouds don't part either. There is no significant beam of sunshine to spotlight the Frontiersman's retreat. Or metamorphosis. One moment he is there; the next he is gone.

Meanwhile, the nationwide manhunt for the Frontiersman is getting nowhere. Phone calls about possible sightings result in SWAT teams storming the McDonalds in Ottawa's Rideau Center, the evacuation of a Toronto baseball game, and the sealing off of Regina's Greyhound bus station. As we know, the Frontiersman is nowhere near any of these places. Instead, innocent bystanders are injured as crowds panic, and the Blue Jays suffer their worst loss of an already terrible season. Facial recognition programs comparing the traffic camera photograph to innumerable databases run day and night but to no avail. Hopes that are raised when the Buick is traced back to the Bingo parlour soon fade. The Bingo's regulars have either expired or struggle to remember what they did yesterday. The technicians' fine-tooth combing of the Buick fares no better. The Frontiersman's relaxed hygiene makes fingerprint retrieval impossible. To quote a lab technician: "Imagine a slimy cave lived in by a slovenly bear with a hoarding disorder."

Unsurprisingly, the Federal Government is also clueless. As with any bureaucracy of its size, it has no idea that one of its employees has stopped coming to work. It not only continues to deposit the Frontiersman's paycheck into his bank account but also promotes him. It is from this regularly funded bank account that the Frontiersman's rent, utilities and other niggling expenses are automatically withdrawn. Red flags remain unraised. When the Frontiersman precipitously left his apartment, his fridge contained nothing fresh, nothing that could go bad. Three and a half individually wrapped cheese slices that would last another thirty years and a celery stalk in the vegetable crisper well on its way to mummification.

The one person who could give the investigation a much-needed boost is, of course, the salesperson at the Ford dealership. For instance, by providing a detailed physical and psychological description of the buyer of the Raptors. Did he have an accent? Ottawa East Side or Brampton, Ontario? Any visible hand tattoos or jewellery? Did he wear his long auburn curls combed to one side, or was it more of a sweep back off the forehead and hold in place with hairpins?

The idea of upstanding citizens helping hard-working law enforcement officials solve pernicious crimes sounds great in theory, but life goes beyond the theoretical. Some people, people who strongly dislike any theoretical or intellectual discourse, even say that life only begins where theory ends. There's also the small issue of the salesperson not being entirely innocent. And the fact that the one-point two-million-dollar sale of Shelby Raptors to a walk-in had transformed his life. See? It'd take one helluva theory to incorporate all that.

"And there's no way I'm going back," the now senior sales director slurs into the ear of a dancer in one of Club Pigale's lap dance cubicles.

When the Frontiersman upgraded from cop killer to province arsonist, there'd been another round of stressful police scrutiny, but the senior sales director self-medicated with liquid lunches at the conveniently located Club Pigale and who can blame him for wanting to conserve the new status quo? Even if it meant resorting to levels of *omertà* that the law takes a dim view of, going as far as calling it compromise of felony.

He'd been promoted that very same day. His own office with a limited edition Shelby Raptor cheerleader calendar hanging off the door and his very own espresso maker. The following week he'd moved from a basement apartment, not unlike the Frontiersman's, to a downtown condo. He'd even paid movers. And there was the company car – a very presentable fully-loaded Ford Taurus – and the dirtiest lap dances his massive commission could buy.

"Mr. Ezekiel was clearly a Shelby aficionado," he told the detectives who had accompanied a furious Mr. Ezekiel to the dealership a few days after the sale of the century.

The detectives showed the senior sales director parking lot footage of a man wearing rubber boots, two different wigs and a burlap backpack.

"Does this look like someone with Amex Centurion creditworthiness?" Mr. Ezekiel had shouted.

The senior sales director calmly replied that he treated all clients equally, regardless of their attire.

"Do I look to you like some small-dicked asshole who needs to drive a wannabe tank to prove his manliness?" insisted Mr. Ezekiel, who, as we know, drove an expensive but subdued Subaru.

Unfortunately for Mr. Ezekiel, both detectives drove pickup trucks as their off-duty vehicles, and both had recently invested considerable sums in either bigger suspension, roll bars or expensive wheel-well liners. The detectives thanked the senior sales director for his time and cooperation and accidentally walked Mr. Ezekiel into the vertical post dividing the dealership's two front doors on their way out.

There'd been some follow-up calls and that visit last week by the same two detectives who came to drink espressos, but that was basically that. Roadblocks were dismantled, the random harassment and frisking of anyone with a beard or body odour ended, and the news cycle moved on to something else. Anything to keep up sales and advertising revenues. Only the province of Quebec, half burnt down and half blown up, entirely without power and crisscrossed by smouldering chasms, had not forgotten. And most certainly not forgiven.

Joseph

In the immolated province of Quebec, basic government activities had resumed since the devastating explosions, but had been moved from Quebec City's no-longer existent historical center to a bidonville of office containers on the city's northern fringe. It was here that the Premier of what was left of the province of Quebec swivelled in his desk chair and took in the hideous décor of his improvised office. The embroidered Fleur-de-Lys flag with singed tassels, his char-broiled oak desk, seating area crammed with two chairs and a government-issue coffee table. The ensemble reminds the Premier of his humble beginnings in government many moons and legislature periods ago. He also thinks his office could pass for a thrift store.

He stands and walks to the container's only window. It is small and provides a view of the adjacent container's air conditioning unit. Only by sticking his head out and looking hard left can he make out the pall of smoke and dust still hovering above his beloved city. If you can call a pile of rubble a city. Gone is the boxy silhouette of Château Frontenac. The central bell tower of Quebec's parliament buildings, a great *doigt d'honneur* pointing both at Toronto and Ottawa, has also vanished from the skyline.

"Skyline," the Premier scoffs bitterly. "What skyline?"

It's true. The city's once iconic silhouette rising proudly from the banks of the St. Lawrence River is now a jumble of debris. When seen in profile, it's not the nose of a Greek or Roman God or someone who has a massive honker but still manages to pull it off. It is the likeness of a boxer with more losses than cartilage.

Thoroughly depressed, the Premier pulls his head back into the office container and, wanting to lick his wounds in the dark, tugs on the window blind's strings. The blind descends, at first evenly, then the left side begins to outpace the right, and soon the blind is wedged crookedly in its ugly plastic frame. Quebec's Premier attempts to even out the blind by delicately tweaking first one and then the other string. The blind doesn't budge. The Premier tugs harder, then outright yanks. In a fit of rage, he rips the fucking blind off the wall and stomps on it. Feeling a little better, he returns to his desk where the first post-disaster reconstruction scenarios and estimates lie fanned out. Fifty to one hundred years, trillions of dollars. His experience in government projects has taught him to triple estimates.

"I will be tree-undred years hold," he mutters, aspirating some Hs and adding another where it doesn't belong.

Dejected, he sweeps the folders from his desk and sits down heavily. History will remember him as the Premier who failed to save the province from annihilation. Perpetrated by a bearded, Anglophone delinquent who is still at large. The Premier who handed *La Belle Province,* Canada's French-speaking province, not its homonymous fast-food chain, over to the English. That will be his legacy.

"Not if I can elp it, heh?" the Premier says decisively.

He reaches for his secure phone and dials a number. Far far away, deep in the wilderness of northern Quebec, a phone rings in a primitive cabin. A cabin to which a phone line was laid at great taxpayer expense. A raspy voice answers.

"Joseph?"

"Martin?"

"Bring me his head."

Nose to the Ground

The Frontiersman and his head are blissfully unaware of this cryptic conversation. That is, if two people stating their names and one telling the other to bring them a head can be considered a conversation. Be that as it may, the Frontiersman is oblivious. Because he has gone native. After the revelation and his bare-boned departure from Kilmar and from civilization, if you can call a paper mill town civilization, the Frontiersman removed all man-made barriers separating him from his natural surroundings.

Here the reader is encouraged to exercise caution and not mistake *natural surroundings* for paintings of English landscapes or depictions of the Garden of Eden. Not even unflattering ones. In fact, there is no link whatsoever between the Frontiersman's surroundings and the term 'land' or even 'landscape.' Had the Group of Seven been trained by Hieronymus Bosch and Jackson Pollock and had used only black paint, there might be room for discussion. But they weren't and didn't, so there isn't. For days or perhaps weeks, the Frontiersman has had the Canadian Shield underfoot. That great slab of granite that underlies two-thirds of Canada and is covered in a veneer of swamp, sickly forests, poison ivy and the decomposing bodies of zillions of mosquitoes. The Frontiersman's bushwhacking has been no cakewalk, and he has become lean. Some would say emaciated. Following an internal compass only loosely aligned with the earth's magnetic field, he advances haltingly through impenetrable brush and dark lakes choked with weeds. Sometimes he lives off the land. Other times, the land lives off him. But mostly, the Frontiersman spends his days with his nose close to the ground, where his food staples, grubs, ants and worms live.

When he is lucky, a skeletal river fish provides fatty acids that stem his diet-induced hair loss. The local flora of untamed thickets, inviolable thorn ramparts, wasp nests and sudden deluges have long ago worn through his clothes. Every inch of his body is covered in scratches, cuts, dirt, callouses and infected insect bites. But the Frontiersman doesn't complain. Not only is there no one around to listen to his griping, but he now knows that trees falling in a forest make a deafening racket and that the only thing that matters is not being where they land. His daily habits are those of all hunter-gatherers. Or gatherers who would also like to hunt but mainly gather. He rises at dawn with the first haunting call of a loon and, after a day spent foraging for anything edible while himself providing sustenance for billions of insects, spends nights in whatever mossy crevice he can find. That's the best-case scenario. He's also spent nights on piles of branches, was buried alive under a lean-to that collapsed and relived the storm sewer trauma in a creek that suddenly flooded. The sketches he makes of his surroundings are his last tether to humanity. These are executed on boulders with charcoal or mud or etched into trees with his fingernails and teeth.

Considering that these dentition carvings are executed an inch from the artist's face, the level of detail is stunning. Has he become extremely shortsighted? Have his gums receded and teeth grown?

The frontiers approached and trespassed by the Frontiersman are not merely physical. The psilocybin mushroom hunting skills he honed in high school help him communicate with worlds beyond our own. He regularly witnesses sunsets involving more than one sun or is mesmerized by a dew-covered spider web or a simple branch. Each is more beautiful than any headless Greek statue or Old Master painting. When he isn't careful with the dosage or when magic mushrooms are his only sustenance, the sight of a simple patch of moss, a weathered tree stump, or the breeze ruffling dandruff from his beard can reduce him to tears and gibberish. His sketches of these events will haunt their non-existent viewers forever.

Another Amazing Day

Joseph steps out of a nondescript car and walks into Gatineau's most successful Ford dealership. He blends into the dealership's ambience of beige wallpaper and off-white floor tiles with ease. The security cameras struggle to record his presence. He asks to speak to the sales director, who only minutes before returned from a break at Club Pigale. Joseph is shown into the sales director's office and closes the door behind him. The cheerleaders shudder.

"Another amazing day!" the director of sales says, rising to greet the prospective client.

Joseph nods in agreement and lowers the blinds that descend smoothly and evenly.

"Number one selling car in Quebec!" the director continues, buoyant after several mid-morning martinis.

Joseph's gloved hand shoots out and crumples the director's nose, propelling him into his executive leather chair in a haze of blood and mucus.

"The guy who used Mr. Ezekiel's stolen credit card," Joseph initiates the proceedings. "Who was he?"

Through tears and a veil of snot, the senior sales director stares at the intruder, who also looks like a senior sales director. But of photocopier replacement parts,

Reader's Digest subscriptions or other goods that don't go Vrooomvrooom and require vast lines of credit. Who else wears matching cream-coloured pants and windbreaker?

"I have no idea who you're talking about," the director mumbles through a heavy nosebleed.

In a blur of motion, Joseph drives the ostentatious letter opener bearing the message *Ford Forever* through the director's right hand, pinning it to the desk. The director's howls of agony get as far as Joseph's gloved hand clamped over his mouth. But no further.

"Delivery location for the first Shelby," Joseph says flatly.

Unlike people who adorn every sentence with breathy inflection, Joseph uses none at all. Instead, he gives the handle of the letter opener a whack. The letter opener makes a twanging sound that reverberates deep into the salesman's innards.

"Tadoussac," the salesperson whimpers. "It was delivered months ago. Has yet to be picked up."

Joseph's next stop is the Hawkesbury marina. When he arrives, the convenience store clerk is in the bathroom, acquainting himself with the latest issue of *Amazing Juggs*. Eventually, the clerk finishes, washes his hands, and then rings up Joseph's pack of chewing gum. He also confirms that the man in the grainy traffic camera photo that Joseph is showing him is the man who recently held up the convenience store. Joseph exits the convenience store and inspects the Buick Estate. The tires are flat, the roof and windshield are now caked in shit, and a family of raccoons has prospered in the upholstery of the rear seat. Joseph opens the back door and calmly slaughters the raccoon family with a folding pocketknife that, when unfolded, resembles a folding pocket machete. Then he gets behind the wheel of the Buick, closes his eyes and inhales deeply. At first, he keeps the air deep in his lungs. Then he does that strange and disgusting thing that people do when they think it's important to aerate wine in their mouths while at the dinner table. Joseph's highly developed sense of smell singles out notes of rot, wet cardboard that's been chewed on by mice, someone living commando style in their car, and Great Lakes Lager. Joseph licks the steering wheel and buries his nose in the driver's seat cushion. He is not squeamish. As a tracker, he knows that every human scent is unique. Vile perhaps, but vile in its own way. Finally, he exhales. The Frontiersman's olfactive fingerprint is now imprinted on the retina of his nose. Joseph walks to the marina's dock and pushes a man who is buffing the porthole of his motorboat into the water. Moments later, the boat with one gleaming porthole is skimming upriver. Joseph stands at the helm, nostrils flaring.

No Metrosexual GQ Types

At that exact moment, the Frontiersman is in free fall. He plummets from the moss-covered cliff he was attempting to climb into the dark waters of the lake below. It is his third attempt at ascent. A belly-flop landing knocks the wind out of him. Wheezing and spluttering, he doggy paddles to the base of the cliff that has also foiled his land-borne attempts at summitting. Undeterred by this new humiliation, the Frontiersman wedges his toes into a promising-looking crack and hauls his skeletal frame from the lake. High above his head, a colony of honeybees interrupts its industrious to and fro to observe the strange but determined frog-like creature far below.

Meanwhile, Joseph has reached the mouth of the Red River. He kneels before a mound of human turds, mostly decomposed except for chunks of cheddar and plastic hotdog casings. Unlike the Frontiersman, Joseph's progress up the Red River is swift, despite his zigzagging course and continual sniffing. Later, while riffling through the unlocked garden shed in Grenville, he's confronted by the canoe dolly's former owner.

"Hey, asshole!" the former canoe dolly owner shouts from behind the double barrel of his shotgun. "Step out of the shed with your thieving hands in the air."

When the former owner regains consciousness in a hospital bed, his clobbered head is wrapped in gauze, and his memory is a clean slate.

Then Joseph is standing in the roadside picnic area talking to Cindy on his cell phone.

"So you're telling me you didn't recently have a good time in Kilmar's picnic area with someone who was bearded. And smelly. Maybe reeked of propane."

On the other end of the line, Cindy rolls her eyes.

"You taken a look around recently?" she says. "This place isn't exactly crawling with metrosexual GQ types. A girl makes do."

Joseph switches to a Quebecois dialect so deep it can be neither translated nor spelled out phonetically. It lives alone on the frontier of comprehension. But Cindy, whose real name is Marie Seguin, understands Joseph. She is told in no uncertain terms what is at stake. The Fleur-de-Lys; the survival of the French language when spoken with a Quebec accent; the honour of Quebec or what is left of it. Marie Seguin swears she knows nothing about no arsonist. Seconds after hanging up, her phone rings. It is someone looking for a good time. Joseph steps over the sodden, termite-infested remains of the Frontiersman's worldly belongings near the blueberry bushes and pushes into the thickets. The Frontiersman's scent is faint but unmistakable.

Elsewhere, the Frontiersman has somehow made it to the top of the cliff. His face and limbs are again severely swollen, this time by bee stings, but he is munching on delicious honeycomb. A breeze ripples the lake below. A buzzard soars overhead. From his elevated position, he sees a break in the dense lakeside foliage where he intends to spend the night. He can't remember ever having been happier.

Joseph is urinating on one of the Frontiersman's boulder paintings. The skillfully rendered inlets of Lac Moulevin and the delicate silhouette of a moose blur then vanish under his urine stream. Later that evening, twenty overland miles through untraversable boreal forest later, Joseph roasts a squirrel on a campfire. The carcass yields little meat, but Joseph compensates by cracking each of the rodent's small bones and sucking out the squirrel marrow. Because of his French heritage, he is not above eating offal and savours gnawing off the squirrel's carbonized ears and sucking out its eyeballs. After dinner, he descends to the water and drinks from the lake. Before swallowing, he runs the lake water across his palette. Decomposing organic matter, negligible traces of two-stroke engine oil, a hint of fecal matter, human or animal but just a *soupçon*. He drinks deeply. Joseph has a stomach like a septic tank. It will take more than a mouthful of fecal bacteria to upset it. The moon is nearly full.

"Enough light to put in a few more hours," he thinks, sniffs the air and vanishes between two pines.

The Shelby

By ten o'clock the following morning, the temperature in the cab of the Frontiersman's still unclaimed Shelby Raptor holds steady at one hundred and seventy degrees. Celsius. The prolonged exposure to extreme heat has made the soft leather seats less soft. Anything made of rubber or plastic, which is to say most of the vehicle, has become a shade more brittle. The tinted film covering the windows has sprouted bubbles, and the truck's candy apple red high-gloss finish is well on its way to semi-gloss.

"It's a goddamn crime," thinks the manager of the dealership, who is standing in the parking lot with his sleeves rolled up. "Who buys a hundred thousand dollars worth of truck and lets it rot?"

Not for the first time, the manager considers moving the Shelby to the back of the lot. When it first arrived months ago, it was the talk of the town. Also, because of the attention-grabbing off-road display the dealership had built to showcase it. With its front tires riding up two big boulders and the rear end vanishing into a pool fed by a garden hose, you'd have to be a hardened Communist not to want one for yourself. At night, the Shelby's powerful roll bar lights blasted into the night, daring extraterrestrials

135

to show their green faces. And there'd been a peak in sales, but news grows old, and no amount of Trinova polish was keeping the Shelby's thirty-three-inch tires from looking faded. Last week a rear fender flair had popped off. The manager of the dealership reaches no decision on the matter of moving the Shelby and busies himself otherwise.

Into the Forceful Current

The Frontiersman is putting the finishing touches on the raft he is building. Pine log frame with a driftwood-slash-abandoned camping chair deck. It weighs a ton, ain't no Venetian Gondola, but it seems lake-worthy. He has even fashioned a paddle from a scavenged plastic cooler lid lashed to a sturdy branch. The Frontiersman gives his creation a last admiring look, pushes the raft into the water and hops on.

A handful of lakes away, Joseph stares at wild charcoal swirls that depict a universe-consuming black hole or the entrance of a nearby cave. He stoops and pushes his finger into the embers of a measly campfire. They aren't warm, but neither are they stone cold. He rises, licks the ash from his finger and continues his relentless pursuit across a ground cover of mossy shrubs and delicate saplings. From a distant tree top, a lone wolverine observes the intruder. Something in the trespassing biped's unerring advance sends a chill through this otherwise ferocious and fearless killer.

Having made himself comfortable in the folding camping chair, the Frontiersman energetically digs his paddle into the water. But the raft's weight is no match for the homemade paddle's branch handle, and it snaps. The Frontiersman pitches from the captain's chair into the water. Once back on deck, he crouches uncomfortably at the raft's edge, rowing with the now handle-less cooler lid. He remains in this position until a back spasm forces him to retire to the camping chair. He swats away the flies feasting on his provisions of rotting berries and scoops a handful of berry-and-fly egg mush into his mouth. The breeze steadies and pushes the raft forward. The Frontiersman reclines in the camping chair and closes one eye. Shortly thereafter, his other eye spells the first eye on watch duty. Then both eyes slack off, and he is fast asleep. By mid-afternoon, the breeze has become a staunch easterly. With a steady hand, it guides the Frontiersman's raft through a shallow strait and into the Mistassini River's forceful current.

The Mistassini River drains an area nine times the size of Luxembourg and is the main tributary to Lac St. Jean, an enormous crater lake formed long ago when something from space smashed into the earth. Little else is known about the lake's creation. This lack of information underlines the limitations of oral history. Oral history is good for retelling events that happened last week or anecdotes about *hammered Bob trying to jump over the campfire last night* but struggles to transmit the entirety of human experience to later generations. Especially, if Bob landed face first in the embers ten years, not to mention five centuries ago. Had anyone witnessing the meteor impact that created Lac St. Jean made a note of the event in their diary before they themselves were pounded into the earth, the written record would at least have stood a chance of being discovered. For instance, by someone who, for unknown reasons, chose to scuba dive in its murky and barren depths. As it stands, Lac St. Jean's heritage, lineage or pedigree is anyone's guess.

Despite the genuine danger of Lac St. Jean being a bastard, the Frontiersman's raft is being carried inexorably toward it. Sheer luck and coincidence keep the raft in the middle of the river, moving along steadily. The Frontiersman, exhausted and malnourished, remains fast asleep. The river's rippling surface refracts the sun's rays and transforms the raft's camping chair into a tanning chair. A fox taking a shit at the river's edge watches as the bright red human floats past. The fox turd drops into the river with a plop, and billions of E. coli bacteria disperse into the current. The Frontiersman awakens with a jolt from a nightmare in which he had erred from his beloved forest and walked into the sun. He has never felt a greater thirst. His sunburnt skin is so taut that he barely makes it to the raft's edge. He dunks his head into the river and drinks deeply. His parched cells feast on mouthfuls of new and virulent fox shit bacteria. Feeling refreshed, the Frontiersman takes in his surroundings. He is aghast to see a cabin at the river's bank. He seizes the cooler lid and tries to paddle the raft upriver, away from humanity's cancerous sprawl.

But the strong current opposes his anti-social leanings, and the Frontiersman's efforts barely manage to spin the raft. He's scuttling across the raft to paddle from the other side when he's laid flat by a savage stomach cramp. He grabs his stomach with both hands. One moment it's as hard as a rock, and the next in the process of liquifying. A geyser of diarrhea erupts from between his emaciated buttocks.

As a hunter tracker of unparalleled abilities, Joseph always pursues his prey with his mouth slightly ajar. Doing this equalizes the air pressure between Joseph's inner ear and his surroundings and improves his already keen hearing. And as there's no one around, he doesn't have to worry about looking like a drooling idiot. He's halfway through another putrid bog when he stops dead in his tracks. He has heard the Frontiersman's terrible moan. It is a unique and unmistakable sound. It is also rare, despite Quebec's numerous fauna crapping into its waterways and defecating into the wells from which cottages draw their drinking water. Water filtration systems in holiday homes, chlorine tablets and bacteria-eliminating UV wands carried by campers have pushed this lament to the brink of extinction. Joseph knows beyond doubt what the sound signifies. His prey is out of commission and, judging by the volume of the moan, also in striking distance.

He begins to sprint through the swamp. The sound of the Frontiersman vomiting into the Mistassini River drives Joseph from a sprint to a faster sprint. When Joseph crests a rise and finds himself on the bank of the Mistassini River, he hears the Frontiersman's voice for the first time.

"Holy fuck," the Frontiersman whimpers. "What the hell is happening? Maybe if I just lie here, I'll feel.... BLARRRRR....ARGGHHHH!"

Joseph dives into the current. The Frontiersman's raft snags on a log. The Frontiersman vomits and shits himself some more. Then the current pulls the raft loose and pushes it around a bend in the river, bearing the now unconscious

Frontiersman with it. Joseph, meanwhile, is navigating a waterfall. The funnelled current rushes him between two large boulders and flings him into the air. He performs a perfect jackknife dive and, upon landing, propels himself forward with powerful underwater dolphin kicks.

Part III

Tadoussac or Civilization's Lust Embrace.

Every day, a blue whale calf drinks 100 gallons of its mother's milk. By doing so it gains 200 lbs per day. Blue whales can live to be 100 years old. Were humans to be more like whales, they would weigh 3.3 million tons at the time of their death. This would make humans, not blue whales, the largest creatures ever to have existed. That adult blue whales 'only' weigh between 100 and 200 tons is explained by their seafood diet and rigorous swimming routine – logical deductive reasoning.

Coons

When the Frontiersman comes to, hundreds of kilometres later and after coincidences that beggar belief in which the current's invisible hand guided his raft from the Mistassini River through Lac-Saint-Jean and down the Saguenay River, he finds that someone is licking his face. He keeps his eyes shut and enjoys being licked. A second tongue joins the first tongue. This is not exactly new ground for the Frontiersman, he'd had a girlfriend in high school with a fun-loving twin sister, but it's still a delectable treat. Then a third and fourth tongue join the licking. His eyelids, the corners of his mouth, the inside of his nose. He sits up abruptly and rams his head against the underside of a porch.

"Goddamn coons!" shouts a voice from the other side of the porch planks.

The Frontiersman raises his head, slowly this time, and looks around. He is sprawled on layers of garbage and surrounded by a family of raccoons. These busy themselves with raccoon activities like compulsively rubbing their faces, walking with their characteristic waddle, or sharing the half-eaten contents of fast-food take-out containers with their new house guest. By peeking through the beer cases and miscellaneous junk that lines the porch, the Frontiersman can make out the skeleton of a bicycle, uncut grass and a street lined with dumpy houses. He helps himself to a moist nacho that has lost its crunchiness and to a generous helping of something that only in Quebec is considered cheese. He feels his strength begin to return. From zero to zero point one. Then his bowels spasm and terrible flatulence permeates the space beneath the porch. Thankfully the raccoons don't seem to mind, and the Frontiersman feels the warmth of unconditional acceptance. He tells his hosts about his raccoon fur hat purchase and how one of their distant Ottawa relatives had saved his life, but the raccoons are bad listeners. He swallows a limp French fry encased in rubbery white cheese and congealed brown sauce and braces himself. His body has accepted the offering. An additional gram of strength returns.

Looks like Shit!

Joseph has also arrived in Tadoussac. He is being carried across the parking lot of the Ford dealership in a custom-built front bumper that is actually a surveillance post. It boasts insulation, air holes for breathing, a comms system, a tube to pee into and numerous holes to peep out of. A short telephone call from the office of the Premier of Quebec had returned the Shelby, complete with its new bumper, to in front of the dealership.

"But this bumper of yours looks like shit!" the manager complained.

"When I cut out your eyes, you won't have to look at it," Joseph hissed before vanishing into his stakeout that moments later was being bolted to the Frontiersman's still unclaimed Raptor.

That same evening the manager of Tadoussac's Ford dealership had a drink in town. An acquaintance comments on the Shelby's shitty new front bumper looks. The manager imagines himself tap-tapping through the rest of his life behind a seeing-eye dog and says nothing.

Keep Moving Scum Bag!

The Frontiersman's convalescence won't be rushed. For an entire week, he hangs out with his new friends, eating greasy leftovers and regularly being cursed and stomped on by the people who live on the other side of the porch. On his first foray out, he steals clothes from neighbouring clotheslines. Months of eating grubs and traversing inhospitable territory have left the Frontiersman lean and mean. This can't be said for the neighbours who have spent the last generations driving to the local diner or donut shop. The stolen clothes are far too big for the Frontiersman and billow around his stick-like limbs. From near but also far, the Frontiersman looks like a scrawny, guiltily loitering drug dealer. A fortnight after being dragged unconscious from the banks of the Saguenay River to under the front porch by charitable raccoons, the Frontiersman ventures into town.

Despite its oversize reputation, Tadoussac is little more than a one-horse with an occasional-whale type of town. But whales are popular with tourists, and the Frontiersman drifts down a main drag crammed with take-out poutine shops, fast-food outlets, tourist trains, tour bus parking lots, souvenir shops and countless motels. He feels like he's in

150

Vegas. A 1950s boreal version of a Vegas that's at the confluence of two mighty rivers. He pauses in front of a diner and watches a family of four whale-sized humans dig into a mountain of deep-fried food. The Frontiersman wonders if Tadoussac's famous whales are kept in aquariums. Should he tap on the glass? The whales feel the Frontiersman's stare and call the manager.

The diner's front door swings open, and the manager steps out.

"Keep moving, scumbag!" the manager shouts.

His time in the wilderness has made the Frontiersman more comfortable with the animal kingdom than with humanity, and his return to Tadoussac's rendition of civilization leaves him speechless. Instead of telling the restaurant manager to free the whales, he mumbles incoherently and retreats into the dark. He slinks along in the shadows until a passing pickup truck with customized dual exhaust pipes emits a beer bottle and a *Fuck you, you fucking bum*. The beer bottle shatters nearby. The obscenities alight on his feelings. Seeking calm, the Frontiersman decamps to a residential side street where his shuffling hooded silhouette causes blinds to be pulled back and doors to be deadbolted. A bowling pin-shaped silhouette holding a shotgun gestures for him to move on. When a police car turns into the street, the Frontiersman ducks into an alley and vanishes.

The Frontiersman's subsequent attempts at social reintegration are no more successful.

"Hire you?" the manager at Dairy Queen asks incredulously. "Who'd wanna buy a soft cone from you? When was the last time you brushed your teeth?"

The Frontiersman runs his tongue around the furry cave of his mouth and wonders when he last brushed his teeth. His best guess is *a very, very long time ago*. He wonders how raccoons get away with eating junk food, never flossing and still having white teeth.

On another occasion, the Frontiersman stops in front of a shop selling fur goods. Fur-lined cases for sunglasses sell for three hundred dollars. Cell phone accessories made from raccoon leather go for twice that. The shop owner taps on the window and, after gesturing at the Frontiersman's mat of hair and dreadlocked beard, mouths, "We're not buying." The shop owner and shop assistant share a hearty laugh. The Frontiersman tries to run his fingers through his impressive beard, but they get stuck in some sort of nest. His stomach growls. Ever since the raccoon matriarch and eldest raccoon sister each gave birth to five baby raccoons, food has become scarce. The fact that the Frontiersman eats twice as much as any other family member has become a source of friction under the front porch.

Just that morning, the Frontiersman stormed away after a heated argument with his adoptive raccoon dad.

"Listen," the raccoon dad had said sternly. "It's time you stopped sleeping until noon. With ten new mouths to feed, you'll have to start pitching in."

The Frontiersman had tried to ignore the lecture by rolling onto his side but accidentally rolled onto five of his newborn step-siblings. These howled in protest, which caused whoever was sitting on the front porch to call everyone under the porch *A bunch of lowlife garbage pickers*. Worse yet, the porch sitter dropped the butt of a still-burning cigarette between the porch boards, and it landed in the eye of one of the newborns. No one had outright accused the Frontiersman of blinding his half-sibling, but voices, raccoon and the Frontiersman's were raised.

"I'm sick of living in a fucking dump!" the Frontiersman had shouted.

"Then go get a job!" the raccoon mother shouted back before continuing to lick the wailing baby's leaky eye that was already turning milky.

Feeling Peckish

Faint with hunger, the Frontiersman rests against a curbside garbage can. With the world spinning, he leans inside.

"Scuse me there, bud," an American voice says.

The Frontiersman inches to one side of the garbage can's opening as an obese hand tosses in a family-sized pizza poutine.

"Whale watching can make you peckish," the obese hand chuckles.

The sound of a milkshake being inhaled through a straw echoes in the garbage's smelly interior. A container with the remaining milkshake lands on the Frontiersman, who is still head down in the garbage can. The lid pops off, and the dregs of the shake ooze into the Frontiersman's hair. A small tsunami of vanilla ice cream, condensed milk, artificial corn syrup sweetener and butterscotch flavouring sweeps into a greasy and dandruffy mangrove.

From inside the garbage, the Frontiersman feels the whale watchers recede down the reverberating sidewalk. The Frontiersman is waiting for dribbles of milkshake to reach his darting tongue when a police baton is shoved rudely between his buttocks. He recoils from the garbage but has the wits to grab the pizza poutine on his way out. The police officer reminds the Frontiersman that dumpster-diving scumbags are not welcome in the upstanding community of Tadoussac.

His exact words are *"Décriss, ordure. Si j'te croise, j'encule ton câlisse."*

With the shuffle of the freshly humiliated, the awkward scamper of those requiring one hand to keep their pants from falling down while balancing a giant Styrofoam tray of poutine with the other, the Frontiersman moves along.

He is debating how much poutine he should eat and how much he should take home to share with his family when something shiny catches his eye. He crosses the street and stops at a free book box in which a book's silvery spine reflects the sun. Imagine his amazement when he sees his beloved *How to survive the Apocalypse* guide wedged between *Be my cowgirl tonight*, a romance novel featuring a long-haired cowboy with impressive pectorals on its cover and a paperback containing the spiritual ramblings of Paolo Coelho. Despite his gnawing hunger, the Frontiersman smears a handful of poutine between the pages of Paolo's mystical mumbo jumbo, rendering it illegible. Then he thinks being safe is better than being sorry and energetically rubs Paolo Coelho's *The Alchemist* against his genitals and into his stinking dreadlocks. He considers removing this shameless waste of paper from the free book box and disposing of it, but garbages have been generous to a fault, and he can't bring himself to deface their stinking, gooey interiors with Paolo's wannabe religious drivel. Finally, he smears *The Alchemist* through some fresh seagull shit before dropping it into a nearby dog turd. Having made the world better, and outfitted with the apocalypse guidebook and a pizza poutine, the Frontiersman heads for Tadoussac's waterfront.

Still Looks like Shit!

Joseph is lying perfectly still in the Raptor's new front bumper. It's another sunny day in Tadoussac, and despite the bumper's layer of insulation and ventilation holes, the inside temperature is easily one hundred degrees. With one eye, Joseph looks up and down the highway in front of the Ford dealership. With the other, he scours the bushes behind the dealership's chain link fence. The bushes appear empty, but Joseph remains alert and continues looking in two different directions simultaneously, despite the headache this gives him. Two stocky guys ambling along the highway stop in front of the Shelby.

"Now that's what I call a nice fucking truck," one of them says.

Joseph presses his face against the bumper box's searing metal sides to get a better look at the two men. Life has taught him that humankind's capacity for treachery is fathomless. Either of these men could be his prey. But one of the two men could also be holding a full-length mirror, which would make the other guy only a reflection of the first guy. This would fool anyone looking for one person and not two. Joseph presses his eyeballs even harder into

157

the bumper's peek holes and searches for signs of disguises, deceit and portable dressing room mirrors.

One guy points at the Shelby's modified bumper. "Wonder what that piece of shit's about." He kicks the bumper box with his steel-toed boot, sending Joseph's head rattling around the interior. Having issued their verdict, the truck accessory critics saunter off. Joseph staunches a nosebleed wipes sweat from his eyes, and returns to his watch, one eye per peephole.

Whales

By wriggling himself into Tadoussac's pebbly beach, the Frontiersman has created an ergonometric reading nook. The box of delicious pizza poutine is balanced on his stomach, and he has already helped himself to several mouthfuls. He opens the apocalypse guidebook at random, chapter twelve as it were, and reads: *Before the advent of Jesus, many cultures believed that whales were divine apparitions.* He pauses to ingest a pepperoni-flavoured piece of cartilage, then, preferring to know what he's getting into, backs up and reads the chapter title. *Survival tips for the marooned, shipwrecked or for crews of industrial fishing trawlers who have been set adrift mid-ocean by cutthroat cheapskate owners hoping to save on wages.* He sighs contentedly. This is the kind of writing the Frontiersman loves. Religion, cultural history, life at sea, large mammals, and the deconstruction of improbable creation myths.

He gazes across the bay at the Saguenay River's mighty current. The same river that carried his convulsing, E. coli-racked body to a welcoming shore. Or porch. The Frontiersman looks east toward Pointe Rouge, where the sun glints off the vast expanse of the St. Lawrence River. At the water's edge, a provincial park information board informed him that the St. Lawrence River reaches an awe-inspiring width at Tadoussac. Unfortunately, countless inquisitive fingers had smudged out the zeros of the impressive width. The Frontiersman only knows it begins with a five. Confronted with this much natural beauty, he decides there's no way anyone would consider a width of five or even fifty kilometres to be impressive. Tipping the poutine container to his lips, he takes a pensive sip of congealing cheese juice. A huge bald eagle shrieks as it swoops across the bay. The trees along the water's edge sway in perfect unison. Given his recent immersion in nature, the Frontiersman knows that the awesomeness of the natural world is beyond comprehension for anyone confined to the human condition. This includes scientists and their satellites and whatever exact measurements these purport to provide.

"Five thousand miles," the Frontiersman concludes quietly, ending the discussion of the river's width. His voice is caught off-guard by the hugeness of this number and catches in his throat.

He looks down and sees he's inadvertently walked into the bay. The toes of his right foot have worked their way through his borrowed secondhand sneakers that are dissolving in the bay. He returns to shore and his prone reading position and delves further into chapter twelve.

A fully grown Blue whale is not only a swimming butcher shop capable of providing a million ravenous people with a quarter-pound burger of whale blubber but can also live to be 100.

The Frontiersman pauses to consider the number one hundred. That's one old whale. He's on the verge of continuing when he espies further zeros that seem to be seeking refuge in the book's spine. Unwilling to settle for anything but the truth, he forces open the book's spine and is confronted with what could either be several more zeros or the previous owner's doodles. Ambiguity at every turn, ambiguity the Frontiersman is loath to accept.

"Can live to be ten thousand or even one hundred thousand years old," the Frontiersman concludes after guessing at the number of zeroes. He shakes his head in amazement at the longevity of earth's largest mammals.

It's no wonder, he thinks, that antediluvian whales come to Tadoussac to mate in its estuary that measures thousands of nautical leagues. His time in the outback has taught him that nature prefers superlatives. Judging by what he's seen in Tadoussac, humans do to. Do the mating habits of ugly brown crabs cavorting shamelessly in shallow puddles attract tens of thousands of tourists each year? No, they don't.

Whales, the Frontiersman learns by reading on, *are mammals like us humans, complete with forearms and legs and nostrils. Admittedly their extremities have withered to ridiculously stunted limbs or have regressed into their bodies, but can you dive to a depth of three kilometres and stay there for two hours?*

The Frontiersman doubts he can. He holds his breath and counts the seconds, gasping for air after a mere thirty. Thirty seconds at sea level. He doesn't have to be told this is pathetic and glances around to see that no one has noticed.

Whales have excellent sight and hearing despite their disproportioned eyes and invisible ears. The text

161

continues. *Their speaking abilities, however, remain subpar and have been described by whale specialists as "someone playing a nose flute." Despite their impressive weight, which can reach one hundred and fifty tons, whales are no match for ships laden with shipping containers that can cut an inattentive whale practicing its backstroke in two. Even smaller watercraft are dangerous for whales. Year after year, there's an increase in accidents involving whales and whale-watching boats. Possible injuries to whales include having their tail chewed up by the boat's propeller, their soft whale snouts gouged by sharp aluminum hulls or being hit by a tourist's chewing gum. You try removing a piece of chewing gum from your eye using only a giant mermaid tail and basically no arms.*

Shocked by the water-borne dangers whales face, the Frontiersman looks up and sees two tourist-laden boats in the bay. They are corralling a pair of blue whales that appear to be breeding. Despite their far superior size, the whales seem incapable of defending themselves. The Frontiersman imagines the whales' shame at having their intimacy trampled by camera-wielding voyeurs. Enraged, he leaps to his feet.

"Hey!" he yells. "Leave those whales alone!"

"Look," a whale of an American whale watcher says, pointing at the Frontiersman. "Isn't that the guy I poured my milkshake on?"

The whale watcher's friends laugh and wave at the Frontiersman. One of the cornered whales emits an anguished call for help. The whale-watching boats close in. The Frontiersman decides enough is enough and scans the beach for a good size throwing rock. Luck is on his side.

Every single rock on the beach is a perfect throwing rock. He rotates his throwing arm to get the blood flowing, then throws the first stone. It splashes into the space between the boats. The Frontiersman flinches. Did he just give a blue whale a black eye? A whale fin appears. The Frontiersman knows that only marine evolution has kept this from being a thumbs-up. Now that he's warmed up, the Frontiersman throws rock after rock. The windshield of one of the boats shatters. Then most of the milkshake-slurping American's teeth yield to a fist size rock entering his mouth. A captain is hit in the temple and topples into the water. The Frontiersman's desire to save the whales has transformed his throwing arm into an advanced missile system. One with a not-too-shabby rate of fire or accuracy. The second boat's windshield goes to pieces. Three more whale watchers receive rocks to the head. The passengers of one boat panic and surge to the bow. The captain orders them to the stern, but they don't listen. The boat tips forward and then slides beneath the waves. Few humans have ever come closer to copulating whales, and mothers shield their daughter's eyes from ten-foot-long whale erections. What began quietly as a whale two-some is now an inter-species free-for-all. An emergency call is received by the Tadoussac police station. *Crazy person throwing stones at whaleboats.*

So Tender, So Moving

Unlike the highly motivated officer in Thurso, the arm of the law on duty in Tadoussac was just handed his lunch through the drive-thru window. Twelve-inches of mixed cold cuts on Italian Herb and Cheese. The officer mutes the call and takes a first delicious bite. Smokey BBQ sauce spurts between layers of baloney and uncured pork pepperoni and spatters the front of the cruiser.

"Fock," the officer grunts through a mouthful of sodium and nitrate.

Whoosh, whoosh, whoosh goes the Frontiersman's arm. If he keeps up this rate of fire, he will soon have moved the beach into the bay.

The trap door at the end of Joseph's bumper hideout also goes whoosh. The Frontiersman's scent trail, until recently blanketed by impenetrable layers of raccoon stench, is dead no longer. Each time the Frontiersman pulls his arm back to hurl another rock, the landward breeze ruffles his unwashed armpit hairs, carrying his scent and maybe pathogens far inland.

Joseph hits the parking lot at an all-out sprint, determination overcoming leg cramps. He hotfoots it down the center line of highway one thirty-eight, then cuts left toward the waterfront. He hurdles backyard fences, blazes across terraces packed with beer drinkers and cuts a swath through a group of apologetic Japanese tourists. When Joseph power slides onto Rue du Bord de l'Eau, the Bay of Tadoussac comes into sight.

Joseph sees someone in the remaining whale-watching boat fire a distress flare. Not into the sky but at the beach.

The Frontiersman also sees the flare. He ducks, and it whistles past. Grabbing the remaining pizza poutine, he retreats to the tree line. Something makes him pause and cast a final look at the bay. What he sees is worthy of the cover of an adult version of National Geographic. Freed at last of their tormentors, the two mating whales breach the surface and perform an extremely rare doggy-style one-eighty. The Frontiersman has never seen anything so tender or so moving. He barely has time to etch the image into his memory forever when the tidal wave caused by three hundred tons of whale plummeting from the pinnacle of pleasure back into the bay blasts the Frontiersman deep into the woods. The tsunami of ice-cold St. Lawrence River water leaves him squeakily clean. He tips the water out of the poutine container and starts walking home. He hopes the raccoons will enjoy its pizza toppings as much as he has. The tidal wave also washes Joseph back into town. By the time he's back on his feet, nostrils sucking in the breeze, head swivelling, the Frontiersman and his scent have vanished.

Again, It Looks like Shit!

Ten minutes later, the freshly-scrubbed Frontiersman is standing in front of the Shelby Raptor. He can't believe his eyes. Can't believe his past either. Did some incarnation of his former self actually buy this overblown piece of junk? He remembers he did, five of them, in fact. Then he remembers that he didn't use his own money, which makes him feel better. Then he remembers his beloved Buick Estate and feels worse. This emotional seesawing takes its toll, and he plops down on the bench of a nearby bus shelter. He notices the Shelby's faded paint, brittle-looking tires and sagging tinted window foil but feels no anger. Instead, he focuses on a small lizard working on its tan beneath the Shelby's massive front tire.

Wanting to even out its tan, the happy lizard rolls onto its back but gets its tail caught under one of the tire's massive rubber nobs. The lizard panics and pulls frantically on its tail. The tail pops off. The Frontiersman emits an involuntary sob. Moments later, a brightly plumed songbird oversees the Shelby's windshield and flies into it beak first. The impact forces the beak backwards through its small head and smaller bird brain. Now paralyzed by guilt, the Frontiersman watches helplessly as drops of oil

166

trickle out of the Raptor's notoriously problematic gearbox and fall into the artificial pool at the truck's rear. The tiny oil spill wreaks havoc on the pool's various ecosystems. Then the Frontiersman sees an inconspicuous man of medium build who just went for a swim approach the front of the Raptor and climb into its bumper. Surprised, the Frontiersman shakes off the horrors that mankind can inflict on the natural world and wonders if he was the one who ordered the bespoke bumper. He thinks the bumper looks like shit. He wonders whether the town of Tadoussac is suffering from a housing crisis. Why else would anyone choose to live not only in their car but in the bumper?

The answer arrives swiftly and brutally and returns the Frontiersman to his former life. Not the dreary government one, but the one in which he was the most sought-after fugitive in the history of Quebec. The Frontiersman looks down at his chest, expecting to see the unflinching red dot of a sniper rifle scope. Nothing. He looks up and down highway one-thirty-eight. No roadblocks, no flashing lights. He waits for the cold steel of a silenced pistol to jam into his ear. For the tickle of a garrote wire to drop around his neck. He realizes he is crushing the Styrofoam take-out box. His survival auto-pilot, which had been on a whale-watching holiday, shifts into gear. Calmly, he leaves the bus stop and begins walking away from the dealership. Then, he moves nonchalantly from the road's shoulder to the forest.

His do-list is short but definitive. *Drop off poutine, scratch behind some raccoon ears, skip town.*

Meanwhile, in the bumper, Joseph has reassumed his observation stance. Arms by his sides, face and nose up tight against the cluster of breathing and watching holes. He has even slipped off his combat boots and employs his toes as wrinkly, linty windmills to push the air entering the far side of the bumper toward his nose. He freezes. There... faint yet unmistakable and moving away from his position is the Frontiersman's scent. He slides from the bumper like something from a sci-fi movie involving intelligent slime and is soon loping along the highway. A rifle case and what appears to be a missile launcher are strapped to his back.

Vengeance of the Giant Spirit Raccoon

The Frontiersman is worried. Twice he's checked under the porch. He's even peeked through the hole in the rotting plywood covering the septic tank. The raccoon family, his family, is gone. It's not uncommon for the adults to be off scavenging or for the older kids to be at school, stealing things from backyards or rubbing their soft raccoon parts against those of other young raccoons, but there's always someone at home. The Frontiersman purrs, growls, snarls, hisses and whimpers. He's far from fluent in raccoon, but he can get by. He can say *Hey! Don't just eat the cheese. Have a French fry too.* He calls the younger brood by mewing and whining.

"D'I miss one of yous fuckers?!" shouts the voice from the other side of the porch boards.

The voice begins to whistle contentedly. The Frontiersman lies still. The porch sitter interrupts their whistling to let rip a wet fart and light a cigarette. Then the Frontiersman hears a sound that freezes his heart. Someone is praying in coon tongue. Praying for mercy. The Frontiersman elbow crawls toward the edge of the porch and peeks into the backyard. For the rest of his life, he will wish he hadn't. Directors of gory B-movies or special effects make-up artists should look at this, not him. There, hanging from the clothesline, are the furs of his adoptive family. Adult coats on one line and ten baby-size skins on another. The furs' former inhabitants lie in a bloody heap on the ground. Steam rises from their still-warm carcasses. Horrified, he watches the newborn with the bum eye extricate itself from its dead and murdered family and whisper *Help us Frontiersman. Avenge us.* The newborn stares at the Frontiersman with its good eye then expires.

The Frontiersman bursts through the beer case rampart and swings himself onto the porch. Surprised, the two porch sitters, seated on more beer cases and rinsing skinning knives, look up. Joseph is five hundred meters away in a tree, steadying the sniper rifle. The Frontiersman stoops to pick up a rock on which someone's written *Hippies use back door* and throws it at beer case sitter one. His throwing arm is warmed up, and the stone finds its mark. Joseph lines up the crosshairs on the back of the Frontiersman's head. The Frontiersman's compromised running shoe disintegrates. It flops open and ceases to provide ankle or any other kind of support. Joseph squeezes the trigger. The Frontiersman pitches forward. Joseph's bullet whistles past the Frontiersman's ear and blows off the face of beer case sitter two. The Frontiersman lands face-first in the pile of bloody raccoon innards. He feels the warmth of their bodies and imagines the individual fingers and opposing thumbs of their little coon hands caressing his face. He leaps to his feet, murder in his heart. Joseph can't believe his eyes. He chambers another round. The Frontiersman can't believe his eyes either. With a single rock, he caved in the head of one porch dweller and ripped the face off the

170

other. Whatever the opposite of remorse is, the Frontiersman is overcome by it.

He stumbles to the clothesline and to the hides of his kin. Overcome by grief, he drapes himself on the clothesline. Joseph takes aim again and fires. The clothesline can't withstand the Frontiersman's sorrow and breaks. The Frontiersman falls to the ground in a flurry of bloody raccoon furs. When the Frontiersman gets back to his feet, one bare, one still wearing a running shoe, he is incoherent with grief. He is also wearing an outfit of blood-soaked raccoon pelts that would awaken envy in any shaman. For the first time in his life, Joseph feels the nip of doubt. Has he awakened some terrible being from the spirit world? He looks through the sniper scope and sees that the giant raccoon has taken a seat on a case of beer and is drowning its sorrows one bottle at a time.

Joseph climbs down from the tree and exchanges his sniper rifle for the rocket launcher. He advances toward the scene of carnage in a running crouch, looking for a clear line of fire. He flicks off the safety. The Frontiersman hears the click of a lighter. Another cigarette being lit? Did he miss one of his family's murderers? He gets up, staggers drunkenly, but his desire to skin someone alive keeps him moving. He shouts incoherently and hurls his empty beer bottle through the open door of the back porch. The movement upsets his compromised sense of balance, and he keels over. Joseph fires the rocket launcher. The rocket streaks across the backyard, buzzes the fallen-over Frontiersman and enters the back porch where it impacts the kitchen fridge, which given its role, should really be called the beer fridge. The rocket detonates. The house, its wooden frame, the sagging living room couches, the linoleum floor, the nicotine-stained drapes, the basement full of a lifetime of accumulated junk and the forty-year-old tar shingles are blasted into the air. The Frontiersman, stunned and with his ears ringing, gets to his knees.

"No wonder I'm hammered," he shouts. "Look what a single bottle of this stuff can do."

Joseph looks through the missile launcher's viewfinder and sees the spirit raccoon stagger into the billowing smoke. Fighting to suppress the first tingle of terror and the urge to look over his shoulder, Joseph stares into banks of swirling mist that would feel at home on the River Styx. The avenging raccoon god has vanished.

Mr. Ezekiel, I Presume

Turns out the Frontiersman isn't as drunk as he thinks. The effects of the beer wear off quickly, and by the time he's speed walking down the shoulder of highway one thirty-eight, he can almost hold a straight line. Only occasionally does he stray onto the asphalt, causing traffic to swerve. His spirit world get-up is still dripping blood and generates its own share of swerving. An ancient station wagon full of locals on their way to the beer store blows past. It honks in support. When the Frontiersman reaches the Ford dealership, he storms through the front door.

The manager is concentrating on paperwork and, without looking up, says, "I can see you're in a rush to buy a Ford today!"

The raccoon god from the spirit world remains silent.

The manager looks up. His overwrought smile vanishes. Ever since the Shelby was delivered and not picked up, he told himself that whoever would eventually claim it would buy some nice pine-scented air freshener and maybe a car wash and be on their way. But he never really believed it. Not since the guy living in the bumper showed up.

"Mr. Ezekiel, I presume?" says the manager.

The Frontiersman nods his fur-crowned head.

The manager hands Mr. Ezekiel the keys to the Shelby.

"She's in great shape," he lies. "Tuned her up last week."

The Frontiersman raises a paw, halting the flow of disinformation.

"There are four other Shelbys," the Frontiersman says. "Twenty grand a pop in cash, right here, right now, and they're yours."

The manager knows this to be true. Ford Canada had ridden the story of the sale of the century to behind the horizon where it died from exhaustion. He also knows the exact location of the other Shelbys and that he's being offered his very own deal of the century. The manager tells the Frontiersman he needs to get money from the safe. The Frontiersman says Don't do anything stupid. Shortly after, the Frontiersman and manager sign papers in the parking lot. Eighty thousand dollars in cash are slung over the Frontiersman's shoulder in an ugly nylon bag courtesy of Ford Tadoussac. The manager hopes to hell the guy in the front bumper doesn't choose this moment to make a surprise appearance. The Frontiersman adds a bloody raccoon paw print to each of his signatures. Then he clambers into the Shelby's stifling cab and turns the key in the ignition. Stale gas fumes pour into evaporation-lined pistons. The Raptor has a seven-hundred horsepower coughing fit but sputters to life. Black clouds of oil leakage, grimy spark plugs and other engineering shortcomings and maintenance lapses spew from its dual exhaust. The Frontiersman is annoyed but unsurprised to see that the tank is only a quarter full. He shifts into all-wheel drive and stomps on the accelerator. With a terrifying roar that consumes at least half a gallon of gas, the world's largest and most powerful street-legal truck bounds from its custom display. It touches down in the middle of the one-thirty-eight with a suspension flattening thunk. The Frontiersman turns towards town. The days of using his turn signal are over.

His do-list is longer than his last do-list. It is also grimmer: *avenge the death of his furry friends, punish the mean-hearted inhabitants of Tadoussac, save the whales.*

Pit Bulls and Wonder Bread

Joseph is standing in the parking lot of Tadoussac's Ford dealership. The Raptor's custom display stand is empty. Not generally of a superstitious nature, his encounter with the death-resistant raccoon god has shaken him. He sniffs the air. Carbon dioxide, nitrogen oxides, a mercury particle or two, raccoon dandruff, Great Lakes Lager. The familiar bouquet lifts his mood. He tightens the shoulder straps of his rifle and missile launcher and kicks open the dealership's front door. Since the business transaction with Mr. Ezekiel, the manager has been in a state of hyper-vigilance. Before Joseph can take a second energetic step in his direction, the manager and the ownership papers of his newly acquired Shelbys have locked themselves into the dealership safe. Inside the safe, it is cramped, and the air is stale, but anything is better than dealing with the guy from the bumper.

Meanwhile, the Frontiersman is in the parking lot of a rundown marina on the edge of Tadoussac, signing a rental agreement. The property comprises a rusted hangar, listing dock and wire mesh perimeter fence. The real estate agent can't believe how stupid some people are.

He says, "Huge demand for boat berths around here."

176

The Frontiersman looks at the dozen half-submerged hulls that clutter the water's edge and grunts.

The real estate agent's enthusiasm infects the real estate agent. "Not to mention the possibility of opening a waterside bistro," he says deludedly. "Who knows, maybe even a casino. The potential here is...." He pauses to thumb through his mental Rolodex of real estate agent superlatives.

His thoughts are interrupted by a rust-coloured car that roars past the marina. It is rust-coloured because it is entirely coated in rust. Several beer bottles and cigarettes are tossed from the car's open windows. Before the jalopy sweeps from view, an unseen occupant shouts, "Pussy! Fuck yearhh!"

The Frontiersman gives the real estate agent a look that says *Will the occupants of that car be mooring their yacht here for a night of blackjack?* The agent pretends not to understand and leans in close instead.

"Closest Gentlemen's Club is in Rivière-du-Loup," he whispers conspiratorially. "Other side of the river. Girls there all got some serious mileage. Maybe you'll want to go the high-end marina, farm-to-fork bistro and table dancing route."

The Frontiersman stamps a bloodied raccoon paw on the dotted line of the rental agreement and hands the agent the ID he found in the Shelby's front bumper. The agent takes a photo of Joseph's ID. The Frontiersman pays half a year's rent in cash and an extra thousand to have the utilities hooked up. The real estate agent tries to remember when the last ferry runs to Rivière-du-Loup.

Then the Frontiersman drives into town to stock up on supplies. Only someone unaware of his plans would call spending tens of thousands of dollars in under two hours a reckless shopping spree. Nothing could be further from the truth. The Frontiersman shops his way down a mental shopping list methodically and with discipline. Only rarely does he add an item that has caught his attention to the list and pretend it was there all along. His first stop is a welding and steel supply shop that he cleans out.

But a man needs more than welding rods to survive, so he also buys a twenty-five cubic foot freezer and a forty-eight-inch stainless steel BBQ. Other basic necessities include two hundred sirloin steaks, ninety cases of beer, fifteen cases of hard liquor, four hundred loaves of Wonder bread and a dozen boxes of tinned mixed vegetables. An experienced outdoorsman, he also stocks up on other essentials. Toilet paper, dishwashing detergent, aspirin and a box of those nice soft earplugs. At Tadoussac's animal shelter, the Frontiersman picks up a pair of pit bulls. He is told they have been severely mistreated and are skittish and violent. He buys two extra long leashes and attaches the pit bulls to the newly acquired and heavily-laden Big Tex trailer with a fifty-thousand-pound capacity. He's already passed the city limit sign when he remembers he forgot dog food. An awkward U-turn causes the Big Tex trailer to jackknife but brings him back to town. He acquires five-hundred pounds of dog food and, never one to ignore a hunch, drives behind Tadoussac's Marie Immaculate High School, where he picks up an ounce of weed and a sheet of LSD tabs. Because it's been a while and is on offer, he also splurges on a rushed front-seat hand job. His one-man convoy leaves town after dusk and via side streets.

A nifty driving maneuver back at the marina finds the Shelby and trailer inside the hangar and the pit bulls outside. With a new and very costly survival knife that had sneaked its way onto the shopping list, the Frontiersman severs the pit bulls' leashes. Instantly they tear around the marina's derelict yard, barking and fighting. He hears them rip something apart. From the hangar's office window, he chucks several frozen steaks into the yard.

"I am now your master," he shouts. "Keep out intruders, and you will not go hungry."

He sets about unpacking the Shelby and trailer. He uses the hangar's indoor crane for the heavy stuff. While manhandling a twenty-four case of mixed peas and carrots out of the Shelby's flatbed, something gives in his back. He staggers around in pain and curses the idiot who thought it'd be useful for a pickup cargo bed to be five feet off the ground. He has a whiskey to assuage the pain. But the pain lingers, so he has another one.

Eventually, he gets his rig and trailer unloaded. The warehouse is a friggin mess, and he can't find anything. After half an hour of hobbling around, he locates the BBQ behind an assortment of metal I-beams, tubing of various diameters, and a towering drill press he doesn't remember buying. Such is his enthusiasm to put dinner on the table that he forgets to remove the plastic wrappers from the dozen or so Porterhouse steaks he lobs onto the grill. Choking and with eyes burning, he opens the hangar's bay door to let the smoke pour out and only just manages to slam it shut on the pit bull's snapping jaws. Eventually, the

179

smoke clears sufficiently for him to see and breathe, and before you know it, more steaks minus their shrink wrapping, are sizzling on the grill. The whiskey has fixed the Frontiersman's back, and a left-behind stereo system is playing golden oldies.

The Frontiersman is blitzed and feels fantastic. He blasts a can of mixed vegetables with an acetylene torch, pours the lukewarm contents over his second steak and folds everything into a steak-veggie calzone. He takes a bite. The combination of unbelievably salty grill seasoning mix, animal blood and sugary vegetables is delicious. Enthused, he empties the dregs of the whiskey bottle over the steaks still on the grill. Flames shoot into the air, fail to penetrate the thick weave of his beard but sear the hair from his arms and set his shirt on fire. Panicked, he rolls around on the concrete floor until the flames are out. He's pumped to find that Pat Benatar's *Hit me with your best shot* is playing on the stereo. He slaps his thigh to the beat and sings along to the refrain. The next song is an emotional Roy Orbison ballad, and the Frontiersman is suddenly overcome by the exhaustion that arises from profound mourning and intense shopping. He slides down the hangar's sheet metal wall, and falls asleep next to the palette of dog food. From the icy depths of the Bay of Tadoussac, a lonely sperm whale accompanies Roy's lament with an otherworldly solo of whistles and clicks.

Save the Whales

Back at the Ford dealership, Joseph is running low on ammunition. Although saying *behind* the Ford dealership would be more precise because that's where he's taking potshots at the dealership safe. Joseph loads his penultimate bullet into the sniper rifle and takes aim at the safe. The projectile chips at the dial's mangled remains and ricochets away harmlessly. Inside the safe, the manager prefers the bullet's high-pitched ring to the rocket launcher's deafening body blow.

"This is your last chance," Joseph says to the safe. "What's the combination?"

The manager would prefer to die in the safe than divulge the combination and look his sure-to-be executioner in the eye. But he has no death wish either and attempts to salvage the situation. He tells Joseph that he's already told him everything he knows. That Mr. Ezekiel showed up at the dealership wearing a bloody squirrel costume, took the Shelby keys and drove into town. As far as the manager is concerned, the cash purchase of the other Shelbys is on a strictly need-to-know basis.

But Joseph is a details guy.

"Did the squirrel say what it was doing in town?"

The manager ponders this. The Mr. Ezekiel he'd experienced was clearly in a bad way. Taciturn and shell-shocked despite his carnivalesque outfit. Ignoring the pounding headache caused by the many bullet and missile impacts, the manager dredges his memory for something he may have forgotten. The Shelby had leapt from its outdoor display. One of the display's boulders had rolled into the lot and damaged several new cars. The slimy pond liner had been flung in the manager's face. By the time he'd run to the highway for a last look, the Shelby had disappeared. The manager knows this version of the story isn't going to cut it. He imagines his tormentor locating the big grinder in the dealership's garage and him seeking refuge from its advancing diamond-tipped blade in the safe's velvet lining.

"Save the whales!" the desperate manager shouts. "The squirrel said it was going to save the whales."

To his amazement, this makes the madman go away. From inside the safe, he hears the missile launcher tube clatter to the pavement. Then the tinkle of shattering glass as the sniper rifle and its now useless scope land beside it. The incessant snuffling and sniffling recede and then vanish. Relieved, the manager tries to get comfortable in the safe. He rests his head on last year's sales ledgers and rations the scant oxygen by breathing only through his nose.

Krill = Shrimp

In Tadoussac's public library, Joseph is seated at a table, surrounded by books on whales. On a notepad, he's written: *As big as three school buses* and *A single whale eats three tons of krill per day.* A book about krill is on the floor under the table. Unlike the whale books full of glossy photos and charts comparing the silhouettes of whales with those of humans, dinosaurs, military tanks and school buses, the book on krill offered only the printed word and thumbnail-size photos of unappetizing see-through shrimp. Joseph summarized by writing *Krill = Shrimp* on his notepad and banned the Krill book from the table. A long multiplication next to this crustaceous analogy established that a single whale eats forty-two thousand dollars worth of shrimp daily. Joseph isn't surprised that many whales are nearly extinct. A glossy tourist office brochure informed Joseph that Tadoussac is world-famous for whale watching. Especially in periods when the river is awash in Atlantic northern shrimp. A plan begins to take shape in Joseph's mind.

He leaves the library and calls the Premier of Quebec's private line from a public phone. The Premier picks up instantly.

"Joseph?"

"Oui, c'est moi."

The Premier had expected more from Joseph. A corpse, severed body parts or a location to which a SWAT team could be sent to finish the job. The Premier is disappointed and gets right to the point.

"I'm disappointed with you, *mon* Joseph."

Joseph remains calm, despite the Premier's condescending tone and his wielding of the possessive pronoun's double-edged sword of familiarity and rebuke.

"He's as good as mine, Martin," Joseph says. "I need a few more days. And some shrimp."

"Shrimp?" the Premier perks up. He loves shrimp. Shrimp smothered in horse radish is his favourite thing about Christmas.

The Premier is on the verge of asking why Joseph needs the shrimp when he is saved by his political instinct. He imagines being questioned under oath. *What were the shrimp for, Mr. Premier?* For once in his life, he wouldn't have to lie.

"How many shrimp are we talking about, Joseph?"

Joseph tells him. The Premier swears. Joseph says it's a small price to pay to avenge the destruction of Quebec. The Premier thinks this is a low blow but agrees. He tells Joseph that he'll have five hundred tons of shrimp delivered to Tadoussac the following day. What the Premier doesn't tell Joseph is that he, too, is headed to Tadoussac. He reminds Joseph not to let him down and hangs up. Then the Premier dials the number of the Canadian Prime Minister.

"Justin?"

"Martin!"

"We still on for Tadoussac this weekend?" the Premier of Quebec asks.

"You bet!" says the Canadian Prime Minister.

The two politicians are arch-enemies, but as they are both politicians, they effortlessly feign affability.

"I've got some good news!" says Justin.

Martin is immediately suspicious and asks what kind of good news. The Canadian Prime Minister informs the Premier of Quebec that the American and Chinese Presidents will also attend the weekend commemoration of the destruction of Quebec-slash-whale-watching cruise in Tadoussac. Martin can't deny this is good news and begins scheming how to use the situation to Quebec's advantage. The two men end their call by saying goodbye in both of Canada's official languages.

The Trebuchet

The Frontiersman appears from behind a shower of sparks and inspects his handiwork. There's little doubt the last weld could be better, but he figures it'll do the job. "She's only gotta giv'er once," he reminds himself and sets down the angle grinder.

He backs up to admire his creation. It's not pretty, but this isn't a beauty pageant. The massive frame and giant throwing arm are made of four-inch square tubing. The sling is a length of anchor chain found in the back corner of the hanger. It's the counterweight that's giving the Frontiersman a headache. He looks at the rule of three calculations covering the wall. If a medieval trebuchet required a six-ton counterweight to hurl a one-hundred-kilo projectile, then a modern-day trebuchet would need what kind of counterweight to send a five-thousand-pound Shelby hurtling across the bay? The Frontiersman chews on his pencil. He simplifies the equation by crossing out the words 'medieval,' 'modern-day' and 'trebuchet.' While wondering how to continue, he procrastinates and converts five thousand pounds to kilograms. Then, on impulse, he multiplies two thousand four hundred and ninety-four kilograms by one hundred and divides the total by six. The answer, forty-one thousand five hundred and sixty-six, leaves him none the wiser.

"Counterweight's gotta be fucking massive," he concludes and gets back to work.

Less than a kilometre away, Joseph is hovering over the bay of Tadoussac in a helicopter. He's in radio contact with the captain of the three-hundred-foot-long factory ship that has just pulled into the bay.

"Dump the shrimp now," Joseph says.

"Here?!" The captain thinks he misheard.

Not every day do you get an order for five hundred tons of shrimp. Much less with the delivery instructions he's just received.

"Do as you are told," Joseph says over the whine of the rotors.

Through the windows of the bridge, the captain of the giant factory ship sees the captains of whale-watching boats shake their fists at him. Compared to his state-of-the-art fish processing vessel, the fifty-foot whale-watching boats seem like bobbing turds. He sees that angry whale watchers have also started gesticulating and wonders what makes people meddle in causes that don't concern them and about which they know nothing. When a tourist combines flipping him off while taking a selfie, the captain pushes the button that activates the sliding doors of the ship's hold and five hundred tons of shrimp sluice into the bay. Its serene waters are soon a foaming free-for-all of hungry whales.

Through his binoculars, Joseph sees an ecstatic five-ton minke whale get fully airborne. It arcs over a herd of famished narwhals and a pack of killer whales gorging themselves. A family of orcas are enjoying the pungent pinkish shrimp sludge until they are elbowed aside by a gang of gluttonous humpbacks. Sixty-ton sperm whales dart to and fro with surprising agility, huge mouths agape. A behemoth of a blue whale, a specimen easily measuring one hundred feet, advances through the all-you-can-eat buffet with powerful thrusts of its tail.

The scenes are recorded by ecstatic tourists. Even the captains of the whale-watching vessels, whose spirits have been dulled by year after year of mostly sightless outings, are enthused. Only Joseph is nonplussed. He has just spent seven million dollars on shrimp bait, and the whale-saving raccoon god is nowhere to be seen. He orders the helicopter pilot to get closer to the action. For all Joseph knows, the raccoon god has changed outfits and is moonlighting as a whale-watching tourist. The helicopter pilot informs Joseph he can go no lower, that the landing skids are already half submerged. Joseph curses and scans the faces of the tourists with his binoculars. He pans from one face to the next but discards one after the other. No one who recently spent months in the wilderness could be so white and flabby. Then he feels that he is being watched. He looks down and sees an unblinking eye staring at him from below the water's surface. It has no eyelashes, is encased in two blubbery lids and must be half a foot across. Joseph tells the pilot to ascend.

"Faaaaaaaaccccckkkkkkkk"

The phone rings in the Canadian Prime Minister's office. Justin picks up.

"Justin, here," Justin says.

His chief of staff, who has forty more years of experience in the bloody and ruthless arena of politics, winces.

"This is Vladimir," says Vladimir Putin, President of Russia.

"Vlad!" Justin says with unwarranted enthusiasm. "Howzitgoin?"

Vladimir Putin doesn't know how to answer the question and doesn't. Instead, he asks whether he too can join the whale-watching expedition. The Canadian Prime Minister ignores his chief of staff, who is vigorously shaking his head from side to side and says that sure he can. With great effort, the Russian President manages a thank-you. Justin says, "Sure thing, man, awesome," then realizes Vladimir has hung up.

In the Kremlin, Vladimir leans back in his ostentatious desk chair and sighs. He could give two shits about whales or a recalcitrant territory with separatist ambitions that he would have squashed long ago. But this whale-watching cruise is turning out to be a mini G7 summit. G8 now that

189

Russia's been invited. Vladimir begins hatching devious schemes. Justin's thoughts turn to what socks he will wear for the occasion.

The Frontiersman is also busy, despite the lingering effects of a breakfast doobie he accidentally rolled in the sheet of LSD tabs. At least his heart has gone from galloping to racing, and his mind appears to have reentered earth's orbit after a lengthy and metaphysical absence. The Frontiersman's mind and the material world are definitively reunited when the ten-pound blacksmith hammer he is wielding lands on his thumb. The Frontiersman drops the hammer and, woozy with pain, leans against the hangar's metal wall. The sheet metal is noticeably cool, and he gingerly surrenders his flattened thumb to its soothing embrace.

It is then that a miracle occurs. Hundreds of happy whales, freshly gorged on grade-A shrimp from Newfoundland's Davis Strait, begin to sing and harmonize in Tadoussac Bay. The vibes of their well-being and contentment radiate from the bay's chilly depths and vibrate into the hangar via its crumbling footings and corrugated metal cladding. The effect on the Frontiersman's pummeled thumb and addled mind are instantaneous. The whales' happiness envelops the Frontiersman's thumb like a compress soaked in aloe vera and an antibiotic ointment made from poppy flowers. On his altered mind, the whale song has the effect of rosé being chugged to chase a double dose of prescription-only muscle relaxant. As the soothing blend of alcohol and narcotics enters the Frontiersman's bloodstream, a great sense of purpose conquers his soul. The tears caused by flattening his thumb with a ten-pound blacksmith hammer while on drugs are rinsed from his eyes with tears of gratitude. For his whale friends specifically, but also for the collective beauty and purity of the natural world. Fine, maybe not for the fox shit-infested gulp of water that nearly killed him, or sleeping rough in Quebec's insect-breeding grounds, or many other things, but now's not the time for pettiness. Through his tears, he admires the towering trebuchet that fills the hangar. It is huge and hideous, an insult even to a Soviet sense of aesthetics, but it's as finished as it's gonna get.

Only when his tears have dried does the Frontiersman realize he has no idea if the trebuchet will work. He figures he has just enough time for a test run, and rubs away a last tear with his purple thumbnail.

He wrestles the BBQ and twenty-five cubic foot freezer into the throwing sling and lashes them together with bungee cords and duct tape. Using the hangar's crane, he lifts the forty-ton forklift counterweight into position. Miraculously, it is a day of miracles, the forklift's trailer hitch slips neatly around the hook of the trebuchet's throwing arm. The trebuchet is now loaded, counterweighted and ready to go. The groan of bending metal and shrieks of tearing welds attest to its preparedness. The Frontiersman reaches for the trebuchet's trigger, a simple metal lever, and can't fucking believe he welded it to the inside of the frame, directly in the path of the descending counterweight. Two of the massive bolts fastening the trebuchet to the floor bow to the forklift's weight and zing into the air. Far below the bay, the whales are distraught by this terrible symphony of contortion and stress.

As operating the trebuchet's trigger in person would amount to suicide, the Frontiersman grabs a nearby empty beer bottle and throws it at the trigger. He misses. He throws another bottle and misses again. He tries again and again and again and again and again and again. Broken glass litters the floor. He pauses to shake out his throwing arm. Then he throws an entire case of empties and nails the trigger. The forklift whooshes down. Like a magician pulling the tablecloth out from under plates and glasses, its momentum yanks the throwing sling out from under the freezer and BBQ. Finding no resistance, the forklift races through the frame of the trebuchet and rockets into the air. It punches a hole in the hangar roof as though it were made of rice paper and disappears into the night sky.

The Frontiersman stands perfectly still. An ancient scout instinct kicks in, and he begins to count one Mississippis. He reaches twenty and risks a peak through the jagged hole in the roof. Night sky and a handful of twinkling stars.

Not knowing what else to say, he says: "Not bad."

Then, and with the wisdom of hindsight, he tells himself it would have been good to attach a GPS tracker to the projectile. How else is he supposed to know where it landed? How's he supposed to adjust his aim for tomorrow? Then his gaze falls on the BBQ and freezer, and he sees that the projectile hasn't budged and that everything about his design is flawed.

"Fuck!" he shouts. "Fucking fuck!"

The ability of four humble letters and their gerund form to summarize the turbulence and breadth of the human condition is unparalleled. Seldom if ever, has language been used with greater passion or economy.

The forklift, meanwhile, has travelled far and vertically into the night sky. On its way up, it wipes out the vanguard of a flock of migratory birds and sows discord among a group of retirees who meet once a week to star gaze. Reaching the pinnacle of its trajectory, it lingers briefly, surprisingly graceful given its shape and weight, then plummets back to earth. When it re-enters the hangar, which it does via a new hole in the roof, it lands squarely on the Shelby Raptor. Its forks skewer the cab, and its massive lead counterweight pancakes the rear end. The Frontiersman, who is relieving himself in a corner, nearly dies of a fright-induced heart attack but is otherwise unharmed.

Finding his voice after a vicious coughing fit, the Frontiersman expresses the thoughts and feelings, the shimmering highs and uranium mine lows of history's geniuses and inventors whose rise to greatness followed countless humiliating setbacks.

"Faaaaaaaacccccckkkkkkkkk," he moans. He clears his throat and hocks a loogie onto the floor. "Facking faaaacck."

Eventually, the swirling dust and escaping engine fluid-scented silence is broken by the cry of a mournful bird. Or the mournful cry of a regular bird. The pit bulls who had interrupted their barking and fighting and tearing at the fence and shitting and digging resume their activities. A concerned humpback whale sends an inquisitive click into the hangar's footings. The shop radio announces that it is five minutes to midnight. The Frontiersman has the night to get back on track. He dons his leather welding apron, lowers the face shield of the welding mask and advances energetically on the remains of the Shelby.

An idea has begun to take shape behind the shield's impenetrably dark visor. The idea propels the Frontiersman

193

across the hangar floor and straight into the trebuchet's metal frame, which the welding face shield has rendered invisible.

When the Frontiersman regains consciousness, he finds that the mighty blow to his forehead has transformed the idea that was taking shape there into a lesser idea. But the Frontiersman has enough life experience to know that not every situation calls for stainless steel and glass engineering. Sometimes binder twine and hope and welds so ugly it's in your best interest to paint them as soon as possible must suffice. He gets to work.

"I Often Dream of Whales"

"Yuri?" a voice in Yuri's earpiece says, "This is command. "Are you in position?"

Yuri, Putin's lead bodyguard, thumbs his throat mike twice. It is code for "In position with eyes on Vlad."

Through other earpieces and on a different secured channel, an American voice says, "All units. POTUS is on the move."

The President of the United States exits the hospitality tent and waves at the crowd. He has eaten four maple syrup muffins and wishes he hadn't. The roll-on tan keeps his indigestion-induced pallor a secret from the probing lenses of the many TV cameras.

Earlier that morning, the Chinese President's jet touched down on an airstrip in Saguenay. President Xi spends the ninety-minute drive to Tadoussac marvelling at this uninhabited backwater's emptiness and unlimited natural resources. He orders an aide to inquire about buying this undeveloped country.

Martin, Premier of Quebec, is everywhere at once. He slaps backs, shakes the hands of people he hasn't taken the time to make eye contact with and laughs with his mouth open as per the instructions of his PR team. Justin is

195

wearing a light blue windbreaker and somewhat darker blue jeans. His dark mane is cemented in place with hairspray. He asks his assistant if he should ditch the windbreaker and go for the rolled-up sleeves look instead. The personal assistant is communicating on two phones simultaneously and nods distractedly.

"Dear friends, guests, dear *Compatriots*," Martin says into the microphone on the dais. He pauses, winces, and forces out a reluctant "and all other Canadians." He squeezes out a tear. "Not long ago, the beautiful province of Quebec suffered a terrible terrorist attack. The Fleur-de-Lis is on de ground, trampled. But rebuilding has commenced and will not stop until Quebec is once again the envy of the world."

"Oh yeah?" a whale watcher from oil-rich Alberta shouts. "And with whose money? Ya fucking freeloader!" The Albertan whale watcher is quickly silenced by two Royal Canadian Mounted Police officers armed with tasers. "That's right," Martin says solemnly. "The rebuilding of Quebec will require thousands of trillions of dollars. When the next ten generations of Canadians see that a third of their paychecks have been garnered to rebuild the most beautiful and bestest province of Canada, they will be proud of their contributions. And Quebec will welcome them as tourists as long as they bring hard currency."

Justin Trudeau pulls rank and pushes in front of Martin.

"And now the whales!" he says and gestures to a waiting coastguard vessel.

The VIPs amble across the sunny lawn and down to the shore. One by one they board the coastguard vessel that will take them into the bay.

A few miles away, Joseph is speeding towards Tadoussac in a Canadair firefighting plane. The pilot has his head halfway out the window.

"Reeks of goddamn pussy in here," the pilot shouts over the roar of the engines.

Six thousand pounds of week-old shrimp slosh around in the Canadair's hold. Joseph's last encounter with pussy is ancient history, but he has to admit that the air in the cockpit could be better.

"Eureka!" the Frontiersman shouts. Eight hours of hammering, grinding and welding have resurrected the Shelby's drive train that snapped in two when the forklift landed on it. The drive train is far from straight, but the Shelby's massive engine appears capable of turning it. The engine is running, not smoothly; there's ticking, spluttering, and the squeal of slipping belts, but the Frontiersman knows it doesn't have far to go. He wipes his hands and face with a greasy rag.

"Doesn't our Prime Minister look great in his windbreaker? Look at that hair! And those snug pants! Yummy! The envy of the world!" The CBC broadcasts its enthusiastic propaganda across the vast expanse of Canada. Tens of millions of hard-working Canadians are too busy working to turn off their radios or change the station.

The Frontiersman effortlessly blends out the public broadcaster's mindless chatter. With his goal in reach and the growing drone of a low-flying plane overhead, he takes a moment to savour recent memories. He closes his eyes and sees the gentle smile of his raccoon mother telling him not to smoke joints under the porch. That a smouldering spliff could set fire to their styrofoam and pine cone bedding. He reminisces further. Although he didn't actually call Cindy when in Kilmar, he imagines the warmth in her voice. No, she wasn't available just now; maybe next time; yes, backdoor action was not out of the question. He thinks fondly of the many times he looked in the Buick's cavernous glove compartment for something, anything, nothing, and how he never came away empty-handed. His thoughts wander further yet, from his past to the imaginary. He watches in surprise as a fox take a big shit into the beer he is raising to his lips. The fox waves at him. Even before the turd's buoyancy propels it into the beer's head of foam, the Frontiersman has forgiven the fox.

Then the visions turn ugly. The fond recollections of a moment ago that resemble nature documentaries with wide-angle drone footage and soothing British narration are muscled aside by nightmarish visions of concrete wastelands and diarrhea-coloured suburbs. The Frontiersman sees himself, broken and bald, in a vast maze of government cubicles. The horror intensifies further, and he finds himself in a coffee shop that roasts its own beans. Its open-concept tables, designed to unlock creativity and facilitate networking, are made from wood imported from Norway. A poster above an assortment of fair trade granola reads *Live, Love, Laugh*. The Frontiersman shudders but manages to order a regular coffee with lots of sugar and lactose milk from someone with radical bangs. His mistake is to also order a large venison poutine. The words die in his throat when he finds himself surrounded by people armed with yoga mats and bulgur salads. They stare at him with disdain and outright animosity.

He dispels the nightmare by turning the key in the Raptor's ignition. Its supercharged V8 engine bellows to life. A male alpha bison, formidable balls almost dragging on the prairie, paws the ground and snorts. The Frontiersman wedges the Shelby's accelerator to the floor with a piece of wood. The engine roars louder still. Has the bison accidentally stepped on its own testicles? Barely restrained by the trebuchet's throwing arm, the Shelby and piggybacking forklift are thrust forward and upward in a pendulum motion. When gravity, which is basically the weight of the entire universe, manages to push the Shelby back onto the hangar floor, its rear tires give off angry smoky snorts. The trebuchet's frame groans. On the Shelby's second run, it flings itself higher into the air. The bison has begun to canter.

A mere stone's throw away, the coastguard vessel full of VIPs motors into the bay. Despite a heated exchange, Justin and Martin couldn't agree on who would use the boat's PA system, so Justin ordered Martin to be locked in the ship's bathroom. Far below the vessel, a giant Antarctic blue whale swims in circles. It was making its way down Canada's Eastern seaboard when it got word of Tadoussac's shrimp bonanzas. Having travelled the eight hundred miles from the mouth of the St. Lawrence to Tadoussac overnight, it is hungrier and grumpier than usual. Its crochety demeanour, titanic proportions and weight of almost two hundred tons ensure that other buffet diners pretend not to notice that it is cutting the line.

"That Plane is Assembled in Quebec!"

As the Bay of Tadoussac creeps over the Canadair's dashboard, Joseph grabs the lever that operates the plane's underbelly doors. He tells the pilot to fly as low as the plane will go. The pilot tells Joseph that the plane is designed to scoop water from lakes and can therefore land on water. Joseph shoots the pilot a look that makes the pilot wish he were a bus driver or worked in a daycare. The plane begins to descend.

Justin clears his throat and, speaking into the microphone, says, "Um.... I often dream of whales." Nobody is listening, but he continues anyway. "Yeah, so... their gentleness and beauty are like totally Canadian."

Martin hears the roar of the Canadair's two Pratt and Whitney turboprops. He hammers at the bathroom's steel door. "That plane is assembled in Quebec!" he shouts.

Meanwhile, the Shelby and forklift are spinning round and round the trebuchet. Each time they apex, the Frontiersman shouts, "Release goddamn it!" Specifically, he's addressing the hook at the end of the throwing arm that refuses to let go of its Shelby-Forklift projectile.

The Antarctic blue whale has waited long enough. It thrashes its huge tail and propels itself vertically toward the bay's shimmering surface.

"Lower!" shouts Joseph as the Canadair skims the industrial zone on Tadoussac's western shore.

The trebuchet disintegrates. For the third time in twelve hours, the forklift pierces the hangar's roof. Although it is the Shelby's maiden voyage, it feels safe with its more experienced co-pilot. Together they rise into the air and path of the Canadair. The collision obliterates the cockpit and Joseph's torso is torn to pieces. The arm attached to the hand holding the hold lever is flung back violently, and three tons of putrid shrimp rain down on the bay. Somehow both Pratt and Whitneys are on fire. The plane nose dives.

Justin is telling the visiting Heads of State that Canadians feel deeply connected with their natural surroundings when the arctic blue whale erupts from the bay's surface. Its timing couldn't be better, and it goes mouth-first into the shrimp deluge. As the shadow of the cetacean giant darkens the coastguard vessel's viewing deck, Vladimir Putin materializes at POTUS' side. With his dead fish gaze, he asks if Mr. President "Wants to talk business below deck?" POTUS, who knows nothing about wildlife, listens to himself tell the Chinese President that the sight of an airborne whale is "a very very good omen. A great omen." It is the last time he will be mistaken.

Instead of rotating away from the coastguard vessel, the whale lands directly on the VIP-laden ship. Its stomach is sliced open by the shattered hull's metal keel, and its blubbery innards flood the sinking ship. Seconds later, the flaming Canadair ploughs into the wreckage. Foreign heads of state, hapless crew, the Canadian Prime Minister, and people whose presence on board can only be explained by their desire to bask in the proximity of power, find themselves crushed, drowning in whale fat, or being hacked to pieces by flaming turboprops. The downpour of shrimp has once again transformed the bay into a piranha tank of thrashing whale bodies, and although largely toothless, the whales' huge gullets and formidable size are enough to keep rescue vessels at bay.

The Frontiersman is experiencing the bitter aftertaste of revenge. His victory whoops prompted by the CBC confirming the sinking of the whale-watching ship faltered when details emerged of the arctic blue's gory demise. Not even live footage of a bay full of happily feasting whales can brighten the Frontiersman's mood. He moves around the hangar, packing odds and ends into a plastic bag. His work is done.

By God and by America

"Defcon One. I repeat, we have reached Defcon One," the former American Vice President who is now the American President shouts into the mouthpiece of his helicopter helmet.

He and senior staff are being flown to a secret location.

"Goddamn Canadians," he mutters under his breath. "Backstabbing, two-faced Canucks. I always knew it'd be them."

"Options," the new American President shouts at his secretary of defence. "Gimme options!"

Deep in Russia's tundra, a herd of reindeer is startled into motion as a dozen nuclear warheads rise from underground silos.

"Which way we point?" a launch technician looking for instructions shouts into an ancient telephone.

The connection with Moscow is very poor, so he decides to do half and half. Six of the RDS-220, fifty-megaton hydrogen bombs, of which only one was officially built, rotate toward China. The other six are aimed at strategic locations in the USA and Canada. Deep below ground, at the in-launch command, a junior officer Googles *Niagara Falls*, a last-minute addition to the target list. He likes what he sees, imagines taking his Svetlana to the wax museum and wonders whether there's been a mistake. But he knows better than to ask.

In Beijing, the Central Committee's emergency meeting has ended. Via diplomatic channels but in non-diplomatic tones, the Canadian government is informed that China will take over the running of Quebec. Or 魁北克.

On Ottawa's Parliament Hill, an enterprising janitor lowers the Maple Leaf flag to half-mast.

"The former American President has been assassinated," the new American President informs the American public from a secret, nuclear bombproof location. He is reading from a teleprompter. His delivery is slow and emphatic. "By French-speaking Canada," he adds, "which has close ties to Cuban Communism. It will be punished. By God and by America."

The secretary of defence has never been to Canada and has no idea why French is spoken there. But he knows that opportunities like these don't arise every day. Not every day are secretaries of defence given the chance to wage war on a vast, basically unarmed nation teeming with natural resources.

"Full ground invasion," he suggests, addressing the President. "Take no prisoners?"

The American President nods his consent and then bows his head in prayer.

Epilogue

Best Damn Book I Ever Read

The Frontiersman is squatting at the hangar's door that no longer opens properly. He is wearing thick leather welding gloves and is trying to befriend the pit bulls. It is not going well.

"Good doggie!" he coos through the slit under the sliding door. A pit bull tears the welding glove off the Frontiersman's hand and devours it. The Frontiersman changes strategy. He loads the remaining steaks into the freezer and pushes it in front of the hangar door. Using a crowbar, he pries open the hangar door. The pit bulls rocket into the hangar and into the deep freeze. The Frontiersman slams the freezer door shut, then welds it closed.

He traverses the hangar's dog-shit-littered yard and realizes he can't remember the last time he was outside. He breathes deeply, but the fresh air struggles to penetrate the stench of singed pit bull still thick in his nostrils. He tears his pants while climbing over the chain link perimeter fence. He widens the tear when he climbs back over the fence to get the plastic bag with his belongings he forgot in the hangar. A cool and not unpleasant breeze aerates his manhood.

F-16 fighter jets shriek overhead.

The Frontiersman walks along the shoulder of highway one-thirty-eight with his thumb out. Minutes later, a beat-up pickup pulls over.

"Get in," the driver says. "World's ending."

The Frontiersman gets in. Between the miscellaneous garbage that has accumulated between the windshield and dashboard, he sees a copy of *How to survive the Apocalypse.* He wonders if it's a first edition.

The driver follows his gaze.

"Best damn book I ever read," he says. "Only damn book I ever read."

ACKNOWLEDGEMENTS

My thanks to Ian Shaw, without whom this novel would exist only on my hard drive. Also, to my mother, Luise von Flotow, whose unabated insistence that I find a publisher resulted in me meeting Ian. *The Whale Watcher's Guide to the Apocalypse* is also indebted to America's many Preppers and Survivalists. Without them, there wouldn't a billion dollar Doomsday Industry, no dehydrated legumes, foldable shovels, or waterproof toilet paper. Not to mention the countless publications, spirited and hilarious, that kept the Frontiersman company on many an outhouse run. And is it true that Wikipedia knows more than God but is better at summarizing it?

ALSO FROM DEUX VOILIERS PUBLISHING

Soldier, Lily, Peace and Pearls by Con Cú (2012)
Last of the Ninth by Stephen L. Bennett (2012)
Marching to Byzantium by Brendan Ray (2012)
Tales of Other Worlds by Chris Turner (2012)
Bidong by Paul Duong (Literary Fiction 2012)
Zaidie and Ferdele by Carol Katz (2012)
Sumer Lovin' by Nicole Chardenet (2013)
Kirk's Landing by Mike Young (2014)
Romulus by Fernand Hibbert and translated by Matthew Robertshaw (2014)
Palawan Story by Caroline Vu (2014)
Cycling to Asylum by Su J. Sokol (2014)
Stage Business by Gerry Fostaty (2014)
Stark Nakid by Sean McGinnis (2014)
Twisted Reasons by Geza Tatrallyay (2014)
Four Stones by Norman Hall (2015)
Nothing to Hide by Nick Simon (2015)
Frack Off by Jason Lawson (2015)
Wall of Dust by Timothy Niedermann (2015)
The Goal by Andrew Caddell (2015)
Quite Perfectly Dead by Geri Newell Gillen (2016)
Return to Kirk's Landing by Mike Young (2016)
This Country of Mine by Didier Leclair and translated by Elaine Kennedy (2018)
Pretenders by Fernand Hibbert and translated by Matthew Robertshaw (2018)
The Fencers by Geza Tatrallyay (2019)

The Marginal Ride Anthology edited by Ian Thomas Shaw and Timothy Niedermann (2019)
The Abyss by Geza Tatrallyay (2022)

Made in the USA
Columbia, SC
29 April 2023

15666213R00120